Dream Destinations

Falling in love all over the world!

This year, you are invited to experience the wonders of Iceland and Costa Rica in Sophie Pembroke's latest jet-set duet!

Prepare to be dazzled by the blue lagoon, hot springs and dramatic landscape of Iceland as Hollywood stars Winter and Josh are reunited once again at the opening of a luxury hotel. Can the memories of their broken fairy-tale marriage be healed this time around?

Available now

And then lose yourself in the sultry rain forest and hide away among the towering trees in a tree house where hotelier Liam and personal assistant Jenny come face-to-face with the repercussions of their one unforgettable night together in Costa Rica!

Coming soon

Dear Reader,

Many years ago, I was lucky enough to visit Iceland for my twenty-fourth birthday, along with the boyfriend who would later become Dr. Pembroke. I remember it as an otherworldly place, quite unlike the quiet corner of England I now inhabit. There were wild waterfalls and surprising geysers shooting spurts of water into the sky and very unexpectedly large taxi bills.

But I also remember it as a beautiful, captivating land. And having pulled out my diary from the appropriate year to kick-start my research for this book, I found that noted in my own hand too. Twenty-four-year-old me was awed by the country—and researching this book inspired the same feeling in forty-two-year-old me too!

I have to admit, writing this book has made Iceland jump right to the top of my travel wish list. I really hope you enjoy your stay there, via this story, and how this magical country brings exes Winter and Josh back together again.

Love and snowflakes,

Sophie x

Their Icelandic Marriage Reunion

—

Sophie Pembroke

HARLEQUIN®

Romance™

Recycling programs
for this product may
not exist in your area.

ISBN-13: 978-1-335-73693-2

Their Icelandic Marriage Reunion

Copyright © 2022 by Sophie Pembroke

For questions and comments about the quality of this book, please contact us at CustomerService@Harlequin.com.

Harlequin Enterprises ULC
22 Adelaide St. West, 41st Floor
Toronto, Ontario M5H 4E3, Canada
www.Harlequin.com

Printed in U.S.A.

Sophie Pembroke has been dreaming, reading and writing romance ever since she read her first Harlequin as part of her English literature degree at Lancaster University, so getting to write romantic fiction for a living really is a dream come true! Born in Abu Dhabi, Sophie grew up in Wales and now lives in a little Hertfordshire market town with her scientist husband, her incredibly imaginative and creative daughter, and her adventurous, adorable little boy. In Sophie's world, happy *is* forever after, everything stops for tea and there's always time for one more page...

Visit the Author Profile page
at Harlequin.com for more titles.

To the people of that land of fire and ice,
where I set this book. And most especially to
Sigurður Hjartarson, for founding the
Icelandic Phallological Museum.

Praise for
Sophie Pembroke

"An emotionally satisfying contemporary romance
full of hope and heart, *Second Chance for the
Single Mom* is the latest spellbinding tale from
Sophie Pembroke's very gifted pen. A poignant
and feel-good tale that touches the heart and lifts
the spirits."

—*Goodreads*

CHAPTER ONE

Rumours are swirling that Hollywood's favourite fairy tale ex-couple, Winter de Holland and Josh Abraham, could be looking at a second chance at a happy ending, as both of them will be heading to the most unexpected destination of the year, Iceland, for the opening of Liam Delaney's new geothermal spa retreat hotel. After the tragic ending to their happy-ever-after last time, we here at LivingtheFairyTale.com had to know more. So we caught up with Winter at a press conference for her nomination for Best Director to find out the truth behind the rumours...

THE CAMERA LIGHTS flashed as Winter stepped out onto the stage, then took her seat behind the table, ready for the press conference to begin. She made sure to smile and turn her best side towards the most prominent lenses, even as she ran through what she wanted to say in her head.

She knew how to do this. Even if she'd never done exactly *this* before.

Winter's assistant, Jenny, leaned over her shoulder to place a file folder in front of her, and she knew without looking that it would contain any answers she couldn't remember off the top of her head. Figures about representation in film, statistics about parts for women over forty, the number of female directors on awards shortlists, that sort of thing.

The important stuff. The things that she'd come here today to discuss.

Things that her first ever big award nomination, as Best Director for *Another Time and Place*, had given her a platform to say.

Winter took a deep breath, smiled her thanks up at Jenny, then laid her palms flat on the surface of the table in front of her.

She was ready.

The first questions were easy—the ones she'd prepared for long before the shortlists were even announced. How did it feel to be nominated? What was it about the film she thought had resonated with the board? Who did she give thanks to? What was the cast like to work with? Especially Melody Witnall, the fifty-year-old star of the movie.

'Melody was a dream,' Winter said, gesturing to where the actress sat to one side of the podium. 'A consummate professional, of course. But more than that, she brought such *life* to the part of Beatrix. She showcased perfectly what I was trying to show audiences—that age is just a number, and that women can find love and success and fulfilment at any age. That we, as women, get to set our own criteria for success, that we can choose our own futures, and a few grey hairs isn't going to stop us!'

That line got a laugh, as she'd hoped. Of course Melody's perfectly groomed ice-blonde hair wouldn't show a grey anyway, although Winter was hyper-conscious of the silver strands appearing in her own black bob. Maybe she'd stop dyeing it. Go grey gracefully, if she wanted.

Or maybe she'd dye it purple. It wasn't as if she had to ask anyone's permission.

'Do you believe in second chances in love then, Winter?' Another reporter shouted the question out as the laughter died down.

Bring it back to the film.

That was the mantra for this press conference. Whatever they asked her about, she just needed to bring it back to the film. The film was what mattered, not her thoughts on love. Or her own experiences of it, for that matter.

She'd had her life hijacked by love before. Now, she was focused on other things, out of the long shadow that love had cast.

'One of the things I loved about the script for *Another Time and Place* when I first read it was the emphasis on the idea that you don't have to be young and fresh to find love. That second chances—and third chances and fourth chances, for that matter—can come our way too, and it's up to us to grab them. In fact, I find those romances—the ones that come *after* a heartbreak—more believable, don't you?'

The reporter shrugged, not used to having his own questions turned on him, it seemed. 'I don't know. How do you mean?'

'Well, in a romance like *Another Time and Place,* the characters are not just older, they're more mature. They know themselves better, and have a stronger understanding of the world, other people, and what they want from both. That makes them more capable of building a real relationship—and that's how Beatrix and Harry are able to find their happy ending. You see?'

The reporter nodded, but the glazed look

in his eyes suggested he'd tuned out halfway through. Winter held back a sigh.

If she ever loved again, it would be different this time around. It would be like Beatrix and Harry—real and private and, most of all, equal.

Or maybe *she* would just be different. Heaven knew she wasn't the same person she'd been the first time she'd fallen in love, eight years ago.

Winter shook her head and brought her focus back to the press conference. She didn't want to be talking about love, anyway. She wanted to be talking about female representation and power in Hollywood—in front of and behind the camera.

Melody fielded a couple of questions next, followed by Sarah, the writer. But it wasn't long before the cameras swung back Winter's way at another question about love.

'You've said that you believe in second chance love—but what about a second chance at *first* love?'

Winter blinked, trying to keep her expression blank even as her heart started to race at the memories of her own first love. 'How do you mean?'

This is not what we're meant to be talking about today.

'Well, your ex-husband, Josh Abraham, said recently that he thinks there's nothing more powerful than first love, or love at first sight. Would you agree?' The reporter raised her eyebrows, awaiting the response Winter just *knew* would be the only thing anyone took away from this press conference. Damn it—and damn Josh and his ridiculous romantic notions. Not to mention his unerring ability to take anything she thought was about her and make it about him.

When they were married, all anyone had ever wanted to talk about was their fairy tale romance—not the films she was making, or her acting or directorial dreams. All anyone cared about was her relationship with Josh. And, in the case of producers, how they could use it to sell more movie tickets. She'd lost count of the number of romcoms they'd been pitched by producers to star in together over those first couple of years, before—

Why was she thinking about this? She needed to focus.

This was her press conference, for heaven's sake! Why were they asking about him? They'd been divorced for five years—twice as long as they were married in the first place. Wasn't that enough water under the bridge to move on?

Apparently not, since the whole room was still awaiting her answer with bated breath.

'I think... I think that all love is first love when it's new. And what *Another Time and Place* shows is that the excitement of love is always fresh and new, whatever your age.' She gave a stock smile, one she knew barely reached her cheeks, let alone her eyes, and glanced up to give Jenny the signal to bring things to a close.

'Last question,' Jenny said, picking on a friendly reporter in the front row who could be trusted to ask something *sensible* about the movie, not the vagaries of love.

But the woman at the back—from some entertainment website or another—who'd asked the previous question, got in first. 'Actually, I had a follow-up. I just wondered if the fact you and your ex-husband will be spending the week together at a luxury Icelandic spa hotel owned by your mutual friend, Liam Delaney, might make any difference to your answer on second chance love?'

Winter gripped tight to the table in front of her and fought to keep her smile in place. 'I don't see why that should make any difference to my views, no. Now, thank you all for coming.' She stood, hoping she wasn't trembling too obviously.

Jenny, bless her, took control in a second, stepping in front of Winter to draw everything to a close, so she could slink off to the sidelines and fall apart in peace and quiet.

'Are you all right?' Melody had followed her, Winter realised, and now stood at her elbow, shielding her from the glare of the cameras, as if they were just having a nice catch-up. God bless other women, Winter thought, as she looked up at her star.

'I'll be fine. Thank you.' It wasn't a lie. It couldn't be a lie. She'd be fine, just like she'd been fine last time. She'd pick herself up again and keep living her life. A life *without* Josh in it.

Everything was absolutely fine.

Or at least it would be, once she'd ripped Liam Delaney apart with her bare hands for inviting her ex-husband to what was supposed to be a quiet week of rest and relaxation at an Icelandic spa hotel.

Then things would be just fine.

'You didn't tell her I was coming. Did you?' Josh turned away from the computer screen in front of him to raise his eyebrows accusingly at his friend as he asked the question. He hoped the twisting turmoil that had taken over his stomach didn't show in his expression.

Liam merely shrugged, before replying in his usual drawling English tone, 'Course not. Didn't want to risk her saying no, did I? I mean, don't get me wrong. You're a big draw, mate. But Winter…she's in another league right now, especially with this nomination.'

And of course Winter *would* have said no if she'd known he would be here. Josh was just as sure of that as Liam was. She'd gone out of her way to avoid him for the past five years. Why would this trip be any different?

It wasn't even as if he could blame her. After everything that had happened between them…of course she didn't want to be around him. How could he be anything except a painful reminder of what they'd almost had and lost.

She probably didn't need him around to be reminded, though. God only knew *he* thought about it every day.

'Who's the blonde on the podium with her?' Liam gestured towards the computer screen they were watching the press conference on. 'She looks familiar.'

Josh squinted. Just on the edge of the screen he could see Winter deep in conversation with the star of her directorial debut. 'You mean Melody Witnall? Heck, you really are out of the business if you don't recognise her.'

'Not Mel.' Liam rolled his eyes and pointed—more accurately, this time. 'Her.'

'Oh, that's Jenny. Winter's assistant.' She was handling the crowd well, Josh judged, as he watched her manage the gaggle of gossip reporters all trying to get access to Winter. It was good to know that she had people like Jenny on her side, now he wasn't there.

She'd run to Jenny when she'd left him, he remembered. It had been Jenny who had helped her through those horrible months, not him. Who'd given her the support she needed. That he hadn't been able to provide.

'She's hot,' Liam said decisively. As if he were the arbitrator who decided such things. Which, actually, he might believe he was. Josh had never truly managed to fathom the man's confidence in himself.

Well, in most things. Not all.

There was, after all, a reason Liam had given up acting and retired to run luxury retreat hotels like this one.

Something else neither of them wanted to dwell on today. Josh let his gaze drift back across the screen again to where Winter and Melody stood. They'd shifted positions, giving him a better view of his ex-wife's face. She was smiling that smile she always put on when things were falling apart but she wanted to pretend they weren't.

Like the time she'd tried to make a home-made dinner for his brother and sister-in-law, going so far as to make the lasagne a week in advance, only for it not to defrost in time for them to eat. Every time she'd appeared in the doorway from the kitchen, unfamiliar apron knotted tightly around her waist, she'd been smiling that smile as she'd assured them it wouldn't be long now.

After three hours and two bottles of wine, they'd ordered takeaway.

'She looks good,' Liam said softly beside him.

'So you said.'

'Not the assistant. Winter. She looks... well.'

'She looks tired.' Josh resisted the urge to reach out and run a finger along her cheek on the screen. There were levels of pathetic that even his best friend shouldn't be made to witness. 'You really didn't tell her I was going to be here this week?'

'In my defence, she didn't ask.' There wasn't much by way of an apology in Liam's voice.

She'd looked blindsided by the question. God only knew how the reporters had got hold of the guest list before Winter did, but he supposed that was their actual job. And it wasn't as if Winter hadn't got other things on her mind.

She didn't ask.

Because she had assumed Liam wouldn't risk them both being in the same place for his fancy press week launch of the new hotel?

Or because she just didn't think of him at all these days?

Josh wasn't sure he wanted to know the answer to that one.

'Do you think she'll still come?' he asked instead.

'I bloody hope so.' Liam paced away from the computer screen and threw himself onto the black sofa that sat against the wall of his office. Josh followed, dropping into the armchair opposite him. Liam really had chosen the perfect place for his office. Through the window, Josh could see out across the rocky lava fields around the geothermal pools and to the snow-tipped mountains beyond.

This hotel was beyond any of the others that Liam had opened in his native Britain or his adopted country—the States. Josh wasn't sure what had drawn his friend to the spa retreat in Iceland, but once he'd snapped it up he'd spent a fortune turning it into the luxurious retreat—an escape from the real world.

Looking out over the landscape now, Josh could almost believe he was on another planet.

'This place has the potential to be really, really special.' Liam sat up, resting his forearms on his knees, and he leant forward to speak to Josh. 'I just need to get the word out. And this week…it's the key to everything. With you here, and Winter, and the press invitees and influencers…we can make the Ice House the name on everyone's lips.'

'As long as she still comes,' Josh said.

'Exactly.'

Josh studied his friend, taking in the new lines around his eyes and the sudden appearance of a few grey hairs at his temples. Liam was only thirty-eight, the same as him, but apparently this was what thirty-eight looked like. And felt like.

It felt old. But then, in other ways, it felt exactly the same as twenty-eight had. Except that when he was twenty-eight he hadn't even *met* Winter yet. And that didn't feel possible either—that there had ever been a time when she wasn't a feature of his life.

'I should leave,' Josh said, the right path suddenly obvious. 'It's not fair for me to blindside her here, when she clearly needs the break.'

'And you don't?' Liam asked, eyebrows raised. 'Besides, I invited you both here because I *want* both of you here. For publicity reasons, obviously.'

Something about his tone, or the way Liam didn't meet his gaze, gave Josh pause.

'Is that really the only reason you asked us both?' he asked, eyes narrowed. 'To get people talking?'

Liam shrugged. 'What do you think?'

'I think maybe you got bored without the rush of the Hollywood scene and decided to try meddling with your friends' lives instead.' Something he didn't appreciate.

Liam didn't rise to the bait. 'Look, if you two are happy, I am happy—especially if both of you can be happy here and raise interest in my new hotel.'

'But?' Because there was definitely a but coming.

'But you and Winter have always been unfinished business. The way she left, how things were before…there was no closure. For either of you.'

In an instant, Josh was transported to that moment, five years ago, when he'd arrived home from filming to their house in Los Angeles and found her gone. His heart dropped again now, the way it had when he'd read the note she'd left.

When he'd realised his marriage was over before he'd even had a chance to try and save it.

'It's been five years,' Josh pointed out, rather than admitting how close Liam's words hit on the truth.

'Five years in which you've claimed you've moved on, dated a selection of iden-tikit blondes—but never for longer than a few months—and generally pined for your lost love.' Liam really wasn't pulling his punches today.

'I have not been pining.' Josh was almost certain he wasn't lying about that. 'It's not like I want Winter back, or that I think she's the only woman in the world for me or any-thing.'

'Except that you still talk about finding your forever love, the one you can grow old with. A love like your parents had.'

'Because that's what I want,' Josh broke in. He wanted to move on, find true love and his happy ever after, with a woman who would stay. It was just hard to do when he couldn't fully understand why Winter had left in the first place.

Her note had said that she couldn't do it any more—couldn't be married to him. And he'd put together plenty of reasons why that was in his head over the last five years, especially late at night when he couldn't sleep. But she'd never explained to him *exactly* what it was he'd done wrong. And, without that, how could he be sure he wouldn't do it again?

Not that he really wanted to say all that to Liam. So he cast around for another way to explain it. 'You never met my dad, but you've heard my mom and my brother talk about him, right?'

Liam nodded. 'Once or twice.' Liam was one of those rare actor friends who transcended that work-life barrier and became family, and he'd spent more than one holiday with Josh's family, especially after the accident. 'Your whole family is as American as apple pie, and about as sweet.'

'He and my mom had the real thing. True love. My brother, Graham, he found that too—you've seen how happy he and Ashley are, especially now the twins are here. They found the real deal. And I'm not settling for anything less either.'

Was that really so much to ask for?

Liam eyed him carefully. 'You thought Winter was your real thing once, remember.'

'And I was wrong.'

He remembered his mother's words, after Winter had moved out.

I always knew she wasn't the one for you. Don't worry. She'll come along when you're ready.'

But he'd *been* ready, for years now. He wanted that settled feeling of home he saw on Graham's face when he smiled at his wife. He wanted that love and the laughter and the warmth he remembered from his childhood home, before his father passed away.

Maybe for a while he'd thought he'd found that with Winter. But he'd realised soon enough that he was wrong. Everything with Winter had been hard, and he'd felt himself failing from the start. And when everything went to hell...he hadn't been able to fix any of it. So she'd left, and he'd let her go without a fight, because he'd known then it wasn't meant to be between them.

Falling in love with Winter had been like a thunderbolt, knocking him out of his everyday life and into a fairy tale where the happy ending seemed inevitable. It had been powerful, overwhelming and life-changing, the way first love always was, according to the movies.

But first love wasn't the same thing as true love.

True love, he knew from watching his family, was easy. Comfortable. When something was right, when it was meant to be, the pieces just fell into place.

He just had to have faith that one day those pieces would do that for him.

'Just…if you're really ready to move on, mate, use this week to prove it,' Liam said. 'Get some closure. Stop beating yourself up for what went wrong and start looking for things that are right. Yeah?'

'I don't beat myself up over what happened with Winter.' Okay, that one *was* a lie.

'Yeah. Yeah, you do.' Liam's smile was sad. 'I know what that looks like.'

It was the closest Liam had come in a long time to mentioning the mistakes he'd made in his own past, the ones that had led to the accident that woke him up and made him leave Hollywood behind. Josh wanted to push further, to see if he needed to say more, but before he could find the right way to do it, Liam was already jumping to his feet.

'Right. No rest for the wicked, as my grandpa used to say. I need to get back to work.' He opened the office door and raised his eyebrows expectantly at Josh.

Josh rolled his eyes and moved towards it.

'And mate…' Liam's blue eyes were bright under his dark hair, falling over his forehead. 'Think about what I said. About closure and all that.'

Closure. Josh imagined, for a moment, knowing exactly what he'd done wrong to make Winter leave, and felt a weight lift. Maybe theirs hadn't been true love or meant to be, or the fairy tale the gossip magazines had claimed after they'd fallen in love on the set of their first movie together and married within the year. But they *had* been in love.

And if Josh was going to risk his heart again one of these days, he wanted to give it the best chance of not getting broken. Which meant not making the same mistake twice.

True love might be easy and right when it came along, but it couldn't hurt to give it a helping hand. Understanding what went wrong with him and Winter…maybe Liam was right, and that *would* help him take that leap into love again.

'Yeah. All right.' Josh stepped through the door. 'I'll see you later. For dinner, yeah?'

Liam nodded and shut the door behind him.

And Josh took the corridor that would lead

him back to his suite—the best in the place, Liam assured him.

At least he'd have a nice place to hang out, while he figured out what to say to his ex-wife when he saw her for the first time in almost five years tomorrow.

CHAPTER TWO

'I CANNOT BELIEVE Liam would do this.' The room they'd commandeered backstage at the press conference, a small meeting room belonging to the studio, wasn't really big enough for pacing, but Winter was giving it a good go. 'Why would he invite Josh if he also wanted me to be there?'

'Because you're both his friends? Because it will be fantastic publicity for that new hotel of his?' Jenny was sitting in the leather chair at the head of the oval meeting table, her long legs thrown up so her feet rested on the surface. The heels Jenny had been wearing for the press conference had been abandoned beside hers at the door, Winter noticed. They'd both clearly decided that this was not a moment for uncomfortable footwear.

She was going to have to spend a week in Iceland with her ex-husband. In the middle of winter.

This was a *terrible* idea.

Five years. In the five years since she'd walked out on her marriage, she'd managed to avoid Josh entirely. Their divorce had been conducted via lawyers and, apart from the occasional cold and clinical meeting on the particulars, she'd never had to have a conversation with her ex-husband since she'd written him that note telling him she was leaving.

And now she had to go to a hotel opening with him and make *small talk?*

How could she possibly do that, when everything that remained unsaid between them was so huge? It wasn't as if she could walk in there and say, *Sorry, my bad*, and make up for everything she'd got wrong. An apology couldn't wash away her guilt, and it couldn't change everything that hadn't worked between them by the end either.

'What was he thinking?' Winter reached the screen at the end of the room, pivoted on the ball of her foot and headed back in the opposite direction again.

'Liam? I've never met the guy, but I think I already covered his thought processes pretty succinctly,' Jenny replied. In her hands she held a stack of worn and dog-eared cards, rippling them into each other with nimble fingers to shuffle them. 'But if you want more insight, pick a card.'

Winter cast a dismissive glance at the intricately designed cards. 'You know I don't believe in that.'

'I've told you. Tarot doesn't care if you believe or not.' Swinging her legs down to sit up straight in the chair, Jenny gave the cards one last shuffle, then held the deck out to Winter.

Winter paced past her three more times before giving in and taking the damn cards and throwing herself into the chair beside her assistant. She shuffled the cards roughly as Jenny said, 'Now, think about what you want them to tell you.'

'How to get out of going to Iceland?' Winter suggested.

Jenny rolled her eyes. 'If that was all you wanted, it would be easy. A few phone calls, and suddenly you've got a can't-miss opportunity here and you're calling Liam to say you're sorry but you can't make it.'

Winter stopped shuffling the cards. She could just...not go. Couldn't she? 'That sounds great. Why can't we do that?'

'Because that's not what you really want,' Jenny replied sagely.

Winter considered. 'Are you sure? Because it sounds a *lot* like what I really want.' Not having to see Josh again, that was the main appeal of the plan. Not having to talk about everything that had happened between them. About the resentment she'd felt, and then the pain and the misery that had consumed the last months of their marriage.

About how she'd failed at the most important job she'd ever been given, and after that...just looking at the sadness in his eyes had broken her over and over again, until she'd had to leave and not look back.

Seeing Josh again, that would be looking back. And Winter had worked so hard over the last five years to only look *forward*.

'You've been looking forward to this trip for months,' Jenny pointed out. 'We *both* have. Remember? Ice yoga. Spa retreat. Geothermal pools. *Massage*. Relaxation and recharging, and other important things beginning with "re".'

Like *reunion*. With the ex-husband she'd never quite managed to fall out of love with, even after she left him.

Yeah, this was going to be a disaster.

Winter put the cards down on the table. 'I just don't see how I can go and spend a week in the same hotel as him.'

'Because you don't make life decisions based on the actions of your ex-husband,'

Jenny said with a shrug. 'It's a big hotel, Winter. You don't have to see him if you don't want to. And if you do…well, that might not be the worst thing, anyway. Maybe it's time for you to get some closure.'

'Closure?'

Oh, God, what if that was what *Josh* wanted? What if he wanted to talk—really talk—about everything that happened five years ago?

Jenny had wanted her to go to therapy. To deal with everything healthily and move on. But Winter had always been more of a 'bury it deep and forget it ever happened' person, and it had served her well until now.

When there was a chance Josh was going to want to dig up all of her carefully buried history.

The history and the guilt she saw in the mirror every day when she met her own gaze. It was easy enough to look away from her own reflection. Less simple to ignore it when faced by the husband she had walked away from.

'Sure,' Jenny went on, oblivious to Winter's terrifying train of thought. 'I mean, you both work in the same incestuous film industry. You're going to bump into each other at events in the future—it's a miracle it hasn't happened already. Wouldn't you rather your first meeting be under your control, when you know it's going to happen? When you can get all the awkwardness out of the way and just move the hell on with your life?'

That did sound better than cowering in fear about ever seeing Josh again. Which, she admitted, she had been doing. And it wasn't as if Josh could *make* her have deep and meaningful conversations if she didn't want to. Jenny was right, the hotel was probably huge. She'd just hide in her room in between whatever events Liam had planned, and the rest of the time there'd be too many people around for Josh to try and get into anything too personal.

Winter's hand hovered over the deck of Tarot cards. 'Okay. So I want to know what's going to happen if I go to Iceland.'

'No good,' Jenny said. 'The cards can't actually tell the future, remember.'

Winter snatched her hand back. 'Then what good are they?'

'Think of them as starting points,' Jenny suggested. 'Each card is imbued with stories and meanings—ones that make you think. You draw a card, or a spread of them, and you look at all the thoughts and meanings there, and you make a story out of them. One that seems connected to your life right now. Basically, they help you direct your mind to the things you need to think about, to consider, to move forward.'

'So it's not really about the cards at all,' Winter said slowly.

'Nope. It's all about you,' Jenny agreed. 'Think of this as a tiny taster of all that therapy you never went to. So, have you got your question?'

'I think so.'

What do I need to consider about going to Iceland?

'What do I do next?'

'Cut the pack in half,' Jenny instructed her, and Winter did as she was told. 'We're keeping this dead simple for now. Just turn over the top card.'

Winter watched the image as it emerged. Naked people rising up from their coffins as an angel played a trumpet overhead. 'Zombies?' she guessed. 'If I go to Iceland I need to know there might be zombies?'

Jenny rolled her eyes again. 'Not zombies.' She tapped one short manicured oval nail against the card. 'This is Judgement. The card of consequences and reckoning, but also of rebirth and metamorphosis. If I had to guess, I'd say it's asking you if you're ready to face your past and move on to your future. Wouldn't you?'

Staring down at the card, Winter replied, 'I suppose so.' The only thing was, she didn't have an answer for it. She'd spent so long avoiding even thinking about everything that had happened. She'd focused firmly on the here and now, on her career, her future, where she wanted to go next... She'd filled her life with so much else that the pain of the past was dulled by the weight of it.

Just *seeing* Josh was going to bring back some sharp edges, she knew that. Was she ready for that?

It had been five years.

Maybe Jenny was right. Maybe it was time.

'Judgement is also about figuring out what you're ready to leave behind, and what you want to take on the next part of your journey with you,' Jenny added, her voice softer than Winter was used to hearing it. 'Maybe that could be a good thing?'

Winter's gaze never left the image on the card.

Closure. That was what she was going to Iceland for. The chance to finally put everything that had happened behind her, rather than just burying it deep and hoping.

This could be her chance to *really* move on

for good—to no longer be Josh Abraham's ex-wife, or the broken woman she'd left that marriage as. She'd failed as a wife, and more. She'd been faking it until she made it for the last five years and now, with a hit movie under her directorial belt and an award nomination to prove it, it was time to stop faking and start living it. Her new life.

She was going to put her past behind her in Iceland this week, and then she would move on.

'Come on,' Winter said, standing up. 'We need to pack.'

The first of Liam's guests were due to be arriving the following afternoon so, the next day, Josh found himself making any and all excuses to hang around the lobby. Now he'd decided to face things with Winter head-on, he found himself impatient to make it happen. Even if she told him in gruesome detail all the ways he'd failed as a husband, at least he'd know. And that had to be better than wondering, right?

So, he wasn't leaving the lobby until she arrived. However lame his excuses for being there got.

First, it was checking his schedule for the next few days. Liam had set up all sorts of experiences and adventures for his VIP guests that week, to showcase everything the hotel and the region had to offer, and Josh had somehow misplaced his.

Unfortunately, the extremely efficient receptionist was able to replace it in seconds, which took away that reason for loitering.

The Ice House hotel had a great coffee shop by the lobby, though, and some designer-looking transparent chairs placed by artfully arranged pot plants and marble tables, so Josh grabbed himself an Americano, a copy of *The New York Times* that Liam had obviously had shipped in and settled himself down in a secluded corner. From his clear chair, he could see everybody coming and going, but with the paper held in front of his face nobody could tell that it was him.

Perfect.

He sat and drank his coffee and watched three different taxis arriving, depositing two travel reporters, three social media influencers and another actor in dark glasses who nodded in Josh's direction.

But no Winter.

'She's not arriving until four, you realise.'

Josh lowered his newspaper to find Liam sitting in the chair opposite. Smirking.

'Who?' he asked, trying to sound uninterested. 'I'm just enjoying my coffee and the newspaper.'

'Winter,' Liam clarified. 'Apparently she and her assistant have just been collected at Reykjavik Airport and should be here in about an hour.'

'I'll probably have finished my coffee and gone back to my room by then,' Josh said. 'But we'll catch up at some point, for sure.'

Liam didn't look convinced. But he stood up and wandered over to the reception desk, welcoming another taxi-full of guests—more reporters, by the sound of the conversation—and Josh went back to his paper.

At least, until another cup of black coffee was placed on the marble table and Liam sat down opposite him again, his own cup in hand.

'This way, it looks like we're just catching up over a coffee, rather than you sitting here on your own, pathetically waiting for your ex-wife to arrive,' he said.

Josh didn't even bother trying to argue the point this time. 'I just want to get it over with. You know? The awkward first meeting.' After that, they could get down to the conversations he really wanted to have.

'I understand.' Liam blew across the surface of his coffee to cool it. 'I really can't believe that you haven't seen each other since the divorce, though. How the hell did you manage that?'

Josh shrugged. 'I've been busy. I guess she has too.'

In his case, it had been fully intentional. After the divorce he'd said yes to basically every project that crossed his agent's desk, until she told him he had to slow down. He hadn't wanted to slow down, though. He'd wanted to keep moving.

When he was moving, he wasn't thinking. And not thinking was the only way he knew to get through the pain that consumed him after Winter left.

But after two years or so that had led to a period of creative burnout, spent lounging around his mother's house in Ohio, watching his big brother lead the perfect married life until he couldn't bear it any longer— especially once he and Ashley announced that they were pregnant.

He'd called his agent and told her it was time for him to get back in the game.

The projects he'd taken over the last couple of years had been more strategically aimed at enhancing his portfolio and his career, showing his range as an actor. It wasn't just rom-coms and action movies any more, which he was grateful for—not least because every romcom reminded him of *Fairy Tale of New England,* the movie he'd met Winter on.

But he'd kept busy. He'd sold the house in LA, found an apartment in New York instead and based himself out of Liam's retreat hotel in the Hollywood Hills when he absolutely needed to be in town.

Winter hadn't been there either. She'd dropped off the Hollywood radar for a while, before reappearing in some smaller, edgier films. The sort of thing she'd always grumbled about never being approached to do whenever they'd been sent another script for a romantic comedy someone hoped they'd star in together. Then she'd moved behind the camera with her directorial debut, *Another Time and Place.* After that award nomination, he suspected she'd find it harder to stay off the gossip radar. With his latest movie making waves too, he was already there.

Which meant the chances of them bumping into each other just went up.

Even if he didn't have other reasons to want to see her, Josh had to admit that it would be better to have that first meeting here, with only the travel press and Liam watching. He just hoped Winter agreed.

Another taxi pulled up outside, visible

through the wide glass fronting of the hotel, and Josh jerked into sitting up straighter, eyes trained on the entrance over his paper. This time, the dark head appearing from inside the car was unmistakable—even if he hadn't recognised Jenny holding the car door open for her.

Winter.

She climbed out of the cab, glancing around her with a smile, and if she was as nervous about seeing him as he was about seeing her she sure as hell wasn't letting it show. Sunglasses hid her bright green eyes from him, but her wide mouth was just as he remembered. Luscious and loving and no longer his. Her black hair waved down to her chin now, rather than the shorter cut she'd favoured when they'd met, but it suited her.

'You're staring,' Liam murmured.

Josh ignored him and carried on drinking in the sight of his ex-wife.

He knew the moment she saw him too.

She was laughing at something Jenny said, brushing her hair away from her eyes as she looked up at her assistant as she turned towards the hotel. And then, of course, he realised that those glass walls worked both ways and that Liam was right, he *was* staring.

And she was staring right back at him.

The happy, carefree smile fell away, replaced with what he'd always thought of as her camera smile. The one she put on because it was expected, not because she felt it.

He was now only worthy of her camera smile.

Somehow, that made him feel even worse than everything else about this day.

Josh got up to leave, but Liam's hand on his arm stopped him. 'The stairs,' he murmured cryptically.

Josh looked towards the main staircase—a modern glass and steel creation that occupied the central lobby, despite the glass elevator that sat just a few paces away. Three women were descending the stairs now, phones out, capturing everything about the hotel, the views, this moment.

He didn't want them to capture him running away from his ex-wife. He didn't particularly want them to witness him and Winter meeting again either, but it was the lesser of two evils.

Probably.

So Josh gritted his teeth, stood more slowly and followed behind Liam to go and greet his latest guests as they entered the hotel.

CHAPTER THREE

'HE'S THERE. In the lobby.' Winter squeezed the words out between closed, hopefully smiling lips.

'Great. Then we get this over and done with fast, and then we get on with enjoying our girls' week of relaxation. Right?' Jenny, holding the door for her, even though she had both their bags too, was still smiling. Damn her. Winter adored her assistant—considered her more of a best friend than an employee. But her friend's determination to always find a path forward, rather than sit and mope for just a little while, could sometimes be a bit much to take.

Still. She was right. So Winter straightened her shoulders and kept walking.

'And the reclusive entrepreneur has come to greet you personally,' Jenny said under her breath as Liam and Josh approached. 'You *must* be special.'

Winter smiled. She and Liam had been close once—before everything—and she was glad that friendship wasn't another thing she'd lost in the divorce.

Even if apparently she still had to share it with her ex-husband.

'You made it!' Liam stepped forward and wrapped her in one of his whole body hugs, the sort that made you feel like the centre of his world for a moment, and Winter let herself sink into it. 'I'm so glad you're here.'

'Thank you for inviting us,' Winter replied. 'I think… I think this might be just what I needed right now.'

She hadn't meant to be looking over his shoulder. Hadn't meant to be staring at Josh, and knowing he was staring back. Hadn't meant to catch and hold his gaze.

But she did.

And she knew in that moment that Jenny was right, and so were her damn Tarot cards. She needed closure if she wanted to move on. She'd rebuilt her life, her career, everything. But a part of her had never shifted from that past she'd run from. It had stayed in that house in LA the day she'd walked out on her marriage.

She'd been afraid, for the longest time, that it was her heart that she'd left behind. That she'd never be able to find love again, because she'd given up that ability when she'd walked out on Josh.

Now, she thought it might have been hope—hope for the future. And she was ready to claim that back.

Which meant facing him. Dealing with him as part of her history—someone who would always be a fundamental part of the person she'd grown into, but one who no longer had any impact or influence on who she became from here.

That was healthy. That was good.

And this was the best chance she was going to get to do that.

Winter pulled back from the hug and was about to take a step towards Josh when Liam said, 'And this must be the lovely Jenny I've heard so much about. I hope you know I'm at your service during your stay here.'

Since Winter had said basically nothing about her assistant to Liam, she raised her eyebrows at that, but he was already reaching for Jenny's hand and bringing it to his lips.

Oh. Oh, *no*. This was not going to be a thing.

Luckily, Jenny was more than a match for Liam's attempts at charm. 'Bag carrier and ticket booker extraordinaire at your service,' she said drily as she pulled her hand from his grasp. 'But it's great that you run such a full-service hotel.' She offloaded the bags on her shoulder onto him and pushed Winter's wheeled suitcase towards him. 'Why don't you show me where our rooms are?'

Liam looked slightly taken aback at his demotion to bellboy, but he took it in good part. 'This way, milady,' he said, flashing them all a cheeky grin as he set off for the elevators.

Winter would have followed, but the look Josh gave her held her in place just a moment too long, and Liam and Jenny were gone—replaced, she realised with dismay, by three young blonde women with camera phones.

'Oh, my gosh! I can't believe it's the *two* of you. Here!' One of the women darted into the space between Winter and Josh and stretched out her arm to take a selfie with the two of them. Startled, Winter let the stranger draw her in with her other arm, aware that Josh was leaning in on the other side.

Because this was what they did. They were celebrities, actors. Public property.

Never mind that they hadn't spoken in five years, that they had stuff they needed to process, in private. Someone wanted a selfie. That had to trump their needs, right?

And not just one person. Each of the woman's companions also needed a photo, and then the receptionist was drawn in to take a group shot. Winter forced herself to keep smiling throughout the whole ordeal, but she could tell from the set of Josh's jaw and the tension in his shoulders that he wasn't enjoying this any more than she was.

But this was the gig. So she—literally—had to grin and bear it.

It didn't stop the memories that bubbled up, though. The same feelings she'd had during her marriage, when it had started to feel as if the real Winter had disappeared behind a facade of the Celebrity Wife people wanted to see. She'd become almost invisible in the shadow of their fairy tale. All anyone cared about was the story—how their eyes had met across the film set, and Josh had turned to the actor standing next to him, who happened to be Liam, and said, 'I'm going to marry that woman.'

The fairy tale was a good story, Winter knew. From their whirlwind first date as soon as filming had ended that day, to their engagement six months later and their marriage just another four months after that. They'd been young and in love and at the time she'd barely noticed how closely the world was watching.

How nobody had asked *her* what she'd said

when she'd met Josh's eyes for the first time. If she'd *wanted* to fall into a fairy tale instead of a normal relationship.

The expectations for their romance had been set so high from the start, was it any wonder they'd crashed and burned? That feeling of invisibility, of their fairy tale being more important than either of them were as people, hadn't been what broke them in the end. But it hadn't helped, Winter was sure of that.

How could they connect, become the people they needed each other to be to get through the hard times when they were both playing a part in a fairy tale?

'Can I just say how great it is to see you two together again?' said the first woman—who had introduced herself as 'Sarra—from SarraSeesTheWorld. The travel blog, you know? Two "r"s in Sarra when you're tagging...' as her friends edged towards the door that led to the spa area of the hotel. 'I mean, you two...you were my first couple goals crush, you know? I was *heartbroken* when you split up. And now...' She beamed at them both like a proud parent at a wedding. 'This is just the best! I can't wait to tell *everyone*.'

Winter's eyes widened, and she could see the panic settling in on Josh's face too. 'Oh, no, Sarra. We're not…we're both just old friends of Liam's so we're both here to support him this week. Separately.'

'Very separately,' Josh added, nodding enthusiastically. 'Because obviously we're still…friends.'

'Right. Friends.' Winter wasn't sure that was at all convincing, but what else was there to say?

Sorry, but you're interrupting our first awkward meeting in five years—please leave.

Jenny would probably have said that. Sometimes Winter wished she was more like her assistant.

Sarra's enthusiasm didn't seem in the least bit dimmed by their denials. If anything, she only seemed keener. 'Well, this is a very romantic place, don't you think? I hope you both enjoy it. We're off to try out the spa. Maybe we'll see you there later? I hear they do couples massages…'

With a last suggestive wiggle of her eyebrows, Sarra darted off to join her friends, and Winter took an instinctive step further away from her ex-husband, suddenly aware that they still hadn't actually said a word to each other.

She'd had so many plans. There'd been a whole speech, worked out in her head on the plane, intended for their first second meeting. About moving on and water under the bridge and closure and friendship and all those things.

She couldn't remember a word of it now. And even if she could, it was too late.

The chance to say it had already gone.

Josh met her gaze. 'Hi.'

Winter swallowed, her throat burning with all the words she'd never said—not just today, but five years ago. Everything that had been eating her up since long before then.

Suddenly she didn't want to say anything at all.

So she turned on her heel, walked towards the reception desk and hoped like hell that Liam had put decent sound-proofing on the suites in this place, because she was going to find her room and *scream*.

Josh watched Winter walk away, again, and willed his feet to follow her, his voice to call out after her, anything.

But he didn't. Instead, he stayed exactly where he was until Liam returned a few minutes later, without Jenny or any of the bags.

'That's the girls squared away in their suite, anyway,' he said, eyeing Josh carefully. 'I saw

Winter on my way out. She looked…well. Everything go okay out here after I left?'

'There were some travel bloggers who wanted photos,' Josh said, his voice flat. 'One of them was really glad to see us back together again.'

Liam winced. 'Ah.'

'Yeah.' Josh shook his head, and finally stopped staring down the corridor Winter had left by. 'This was a mistake. Both of us being here. I shouldn't have come—or I should have left yesterday, when I realised you hadn't told her I'd be here.'

'No, no, you shouldn't.' Taking his elbow, Liam led him back to the seats they'd occupied earlier. 'Come on. You knew that first meeting was going to be difficult.'

'And you left me here to deal with it alone, in public, while you chased after your latest hot blonde.' The accusation came out without thinking, and Josh regretted it the moment he'd said it, even before he saw the pain that flashed across Liam's face.

Because Liam *didn't* chase hot blondes any more. Oh, he flirted, he charmed, he sweet-talked. But then he left them at the door, went home alone and never, ever called them. And Josh knew that.

'That assistant of Winter's has a way of

making you do things without even realising you've agreed,' Liam said mildly. 'I *am* sorry for leaving you, though. I didn't mean to.'

'It's okay. Jenny always was a force of nature.' That had been something of a comfort, actually, when Winter left. That at least she wasn't alone—she had Jenny on her side. And that was worth a lot. 'It was just unfortunate that those influencers happened to come down right then.'

'So maybe you need to make sure that your next meeting is more private?' Liam suggested. 'There's plenty of quiet, secluded corners around this place. Just drop her a line via Reception and ask her to meet you someplace, maybe?'

'Maybe.' It wasn't a *bad* idea—they did need to talk, after all, before their next public appearance, ideally. He just wasn't sure what he'd do if her answer was a flat no.

Liam clapped a hand against Josh's shoulder. 'Go on. Head back to your room. Go for a soak in that *stunning* private geothermal pool outside your suite. Relax a bit and think about it. Okay?'

The geothermal pool did sound nice. Liam had given him one of the best suites in the place, and Josh certainly intended to make the most of it. And thinking…that was definitely something he needed to do.

'Yeah, okay.'

He managed to avoid any other guests as he made his way back to his room, but he couldn't avoid his own thoughts. He couldn't deny how seeing Winter again had affected him, not now there was no one else to distract him.

She was still so beautiful. When her eyes had met his, their gazes locked, he'd felt the same damn way he had on that film set eight years ago. The same rush of unnameable feelings running through him—some mix of excitement, anticipation, attraction, nerves and…home.

Except Winter wasn't his home any more. She wasn't his anything.

How was he supposed to find closure, to close the door on that part of his life and move on, when he still wanted her in his arms so badly?

Josh reached his door and let himself in with a sigh of relief when the key card worked first time.

His suite was on the ground floor, at the back of the hotel, and comprised of a bedroom, en suite bathroom and sitting room with sofa, coffee table, desk and a coffee machine. The Scandi-style design was soothing, with its pale grey walls, darker grey textiles and the warm wood of the furniture. Against the outside wall, there was even a wood-burning heater, to guard against the February chill.

Full-length glass doors looked out over the white tips of the mountains in the distance, the earthy colours of the rocky terrain around the hotel and the bright blue of the private geothermal lagoon just outside, surrounded by a wooden decked terrace with pale bean-bag chairs around it.

He had to admire the attention to detail Liam had put into the place. It was the perfect place to relax and recharge.

Or it would be, if it wasn't for the screaming he could hear through the wall of the suite next door.

The screaming felt good, but it didn't really solve anything and Winter's throat was getting sore, so eventually she stopped, put her hands on her hips and stared out of the full-length glass doors at the view of the mountains and the private geothermal lagoon Liam had promised her to go with her suite when he'd been persuading her to come.

Jenny, sitting on the sofa of their two-bedroom suite, cautiously removed her ear-plugs. 'You're quiet. It's making me nervous.'

'I'm thinking.'

'That only makes it worse.' Jenny stood up and came to stand beside her, looking out of the window. 'Okay, so what are we thinking?'

'I'm thinking that the screaming hasn't helped, so I'm going to go try out the geo-thermal lagoon instead.'

'Good idea,' Jenny said. 'Your swimsuits are in the top drawer on the left of the dresser in your room.'

It was kind of sad how much she relied on Jenny these days, Winter mused as she changed into a black two-piece that was held up by a single strap and some hope. An assistant was meant to assist, but some days Winter wondered if she'd just fall apart without her.

She grabbed a fluffy ice-white towel from the stack in the oversized en suite bathroom and headed back out into the living area, surprised to see Jenny still fully dressed, with her laptop out, replying to a text on her phone. 'Aren't you coming?'

Her assistant shook her head and slipped her phone into her pocket. 'Actually, I'm going to go find a quiet spot with good coffee to catch up on some emails.'

'Work?' Winter frowned. 'Do you need me?'

'I got it. You go soak.' Packing up her laptop, Jenny headed for the door, leaving Winter alone.

Alone with a geothermal lagoon. That was the sort of alone she could get behind.

Slipping into the luxurious bathrobe provided for the purpose, along with the matching sliders for her feet, Winter stepped out through the glass doors and onto the decking. In the cold winter air her exposed skin puckered with goosebumps—but she could see steam rising from the small private lagoon. Its waters seemed absurdly blue, and a faintly sulphurous smell rose from them. Around her, a faint fog filled the air—the meeting of the warm water and the freezing atmosphere, she assumed.

It felt oddly otherworldly here, looking out over such unfamiliar terrain. She glanced back at the doors of her suite for reassurance that she hadn't suddenly been transported to another planet somehow—and spotted movement behind the doors of the adjoining suite.

Liam hadn't said she'd be sharing the private lagoon with anybody. Who could be in there?

The doors to the next-door suite slid open

and she got her answer—even if she rather regretted asking the question.

'Hello, Winter,' Josh said, an apologetic smile on his face. He was still dressed in the clothes he'd had on earlier and held his hands out in a supplicant gesture.

She stared at him for a long moment, trying to find an answer, her anger at least keeping her warm. Not only had Liam not told her that her ex-husband would be here this week, he'd actually put him in the adjoining suite to her.

'I'm going to kill Liam,' she muttered. Then, because it was bloody cold and this was *her* private lagoon, thank you, she shucked off her bathrobe and stepped into the water.

She thought for a second she heard a sharp intake of breath from him at the sight of her bikini. But if she did it was quickly lost behind the sound of her own gasp as she submerged herself in the water.

It was *warm*. Not just 'not freezing' swimming pool water, like she'd half expected. Properly warm. And wonderful. Like a bath. Her eyes fluttered closed as she settled herself against the smooth rock, her arms hooked back over the rim to support her as she floated.

It almost made her feel as if she could forget all about her ex-husband and soon-to-be-ex-friend if she could just stay in this water for ever.

'It's pretty incredible, huh?'

She opened her eyes at Josh's voice and found him perched on the edge of one of the recliners on the decking that surrounded the lagoon.

'You've been in already?' she asked.

Josh nodded. 'I've been here a few days. I… I'm sorry. I didn't realise Liam hadn't told you I'd be here until I saw your press conference yesterday.'

Winter started in surprise, almost losing her balance against the rock. 'You watched my press conference?' She'd already guessed that Liam wouldn't have told him. Josh had gone out of his way over the past five years to avoid her at all turns. But the press conference comment caught her off-guard.

He flashed her a quick smile—the one that graced movie posters across the world, and probably quite a few phone wallpapers. 'Of course I watched it. Best Director nomination? Winter, that's incredible. Of course I watched.'

The warmth that filled her chest was entirely due to the geothermal properties of the lagoon, she was certain. Just like the ache that matched it probably had something to do with the rocks.

Neither had anything to do with the man smiling at her, or the pride in his voice. His recognition of everything she'd worked so hard for since they'd parted. Or the fact that this was the first civil conversation they'd managed in years.

Almost as if he'd forgiven her for everything. Almost as if she'd forgotten everything that needed forgiving. Both things, of course, were impossible.

'So, what do you think Liam is playing at, then?' She'd meant it as an attempt to change the subject, to get away from all that heart-clenching feeling. But of course it only made things worse.

'Matchmaker, probably.' The twist of Josh's mouth told her he wasn't any happier about this than she was. 'God knows why. It's not exactly like him. But since the accident...'

'Yeah,' she agreed as he trailed off. 'Something like that changes a person, I guess.'

Another guilt to add to her list—not supporting Liam through his hard times. She was a bad friend, as well as a bad wife and a bad—well. Most things.

But she was a good director. She had the nomination to prove it. And Winter had always believed in building on her strengths rather than dwelling on her failings.

'So. How do you want to manage this?' Josh asked. 'I can always ask Liam for another room, if you'd like me to move? Although I think the hotel is pretty packed this week…'

Of course it was. This was Liam's big press week—one week of splashing out to put up stars and reporters and influencers, showing them everything there was to love about his new venture, then hoping their social proof of how great it was would bring the bookings rolling in.

Winter knew that she and Josh were here as the faces of the brand, every bit as much as Liam's friends. They'd both invested in his company from the start, so had their own interests in the hotel being a success.

Which meant supporting him. And, apparently, putting up with his matchmaking. However frustrating it was.

And she'd come here for closure, hadn't she? For the chance to move on.

Maybe the forgetting part was impossible. But could forgiveness be within their reach?

Winter knew she'd done plenty that she needed to ask forgiveness for, even if there were some things for which she'd never be able to forgive herself. And Josh…maybe he needed some closure too.

Maybe they could both find what they needed this weekend and be able to move on. If they were willing to face down the demons that had driven them apart five years ago.

Winter swallowed and made her decision.

CHAPTER FOUR

JOSH WAS ALL set to go pack his bags from the look on Winter's face, until her annoyance turned to something that looked more like frustration and she shook her head.

'No. There's no point.' She kicked her feet under the water, and Josh tried not to stare at the acres of bare skin her bikini showed off. It wasn't his skin to stare at any more, even if it was so incredibly close and tempting.

I want closure. I can't want her too.

'Liam would only have to move another guest into that suite to move you out, and then I'd have to share this beautiful lagoon with someone I don't even know.'

It was on the tip of his tongue to suggest that he could move into Liam's suite with him, even though he really didn't want to, when Winter spoke again, surprising him.

'And besides. Maybe this could be...good.'

'Good?' Josh concentrated hard on not just

falling into the pool in shock at her calling anything to do with him 'good'. Almost as if she'd forgotten all the awfulness that had passed between them. How badly he'd failed her as a husband. How he'd driven her away. 'Good...how, exactly?'

Winter shrugged, the water rippling around her and her luscious body bobbing in the waves. Five years on, she was still the most beautiful woman he'd ever seen. Still the woman he'd fallen head over heels for, so in love he hadn't been able to see straight.

'I guess...we're both here all week, right? And it has been suggested to me that our relationship ended without the sort of...' She pulled a face as she fumbled for the word she wanted.

'Closure?' Josh guessed, remembering his conversation with Liam.

'Exactly. Without the sort of closure we might need to move on effectively and healthily. Emotion-wise, I guess.' She shrugged again. 'Jenny wasn't entirely clear on that point.'

'Neither was Liam,' Josh admitted. 'But you're making me think that perhaps the room assignments weren't actually matchmaking. More...mending?'

'Match-mending? You know that's not a

thing, right?' Winter laughed, and the sound echoed off the rocks around them like rainbow light in a prism. 'No, I get what you mean, though. You think he's trying to make us make up as friends?'

Josh nodded. 'I think so. He pointed out that things between us were left rather unresolved when you—' He broke off. He didn't want to cast blame around here. God knew, enough of it had landed on his shoulders anyway.

'When I walked out.' It was as though a cloud had crossed the sun, the way the laughter fell from her face. 'Yeah. He's right.'

'I think he was hoping we'd talk, at least,' Josh offered. 'Find some answers about what went wrong so that next time we can get it right.'

Winter's obvious surprise sent her eyebrows flying towards her hairline. 'Next time?'

'With whoever each of us falls in love with next,' he clarified hurriedly. 'I mean, as a way for us to move on from each other. Because I don't know about you but…the divorce left me a little wary of love.' To put it mildly.

He wanted to find the sort of love his parents had shared, that his brother had found. But not knowing what he'd got so wrong last time…it was hard to take the risk of it all happening again.

It would hurt, Josh knew, to face everything that had happened between him and Winter. Especially to relive that terrifying, heartbreaking last few months they'd been together.

But it would hurt more to never move on from it at all.

'So now you're ready to get back out there again? Find Mrs Abraham number two?' She smiled as she said it, the idea of him dropping the torch he'd kept gripping hold of for her and moving onto someone new obviously a good one in her mind.

As it should be in his. It was just easier to remember that when she wasn't right in front of him. Wearing a swimsuit that only highlighted those curves he'd once loved. And held. And caressed…

'You kept your name,' he pointed out, looking away. 'So she'd have to be Mrs Abraham number one.' Except that was his mother, or maybe his sister-in-law, Ashley.

'I suppose so,' Winter said with a brittle smile. 'The point is, closure, right? We talk and we move on.'

'That seems to be Liam's plan.'

'In which case, it makes sense for us both to stay here,' Winter said. 'It's probably the most private spot in the whole place for us to talk and… I don't know about you, but I'd rather not be overheard having these conversations. In case you haven't noticed, this whole hotel is teeming with gossip journalists, travel reporters and social media stars.'

'Who would happily broadcast our cosy conversations and lunch dates to the world.' Josh sighed. 'You're right. If we're going to do this, we want it to be private.'

He couldn't take all those stories again, speculating on his broken heart, or his prospects now he was single.

'Definitely,' Winter said with an enthusiastic nod. 'So…we keep them here?'

'And when we're out in public, with everyone watching, we…what?' Josh asked. 'Pretend like we hate each other?'

'I don't think we need to go that far.' Winter shifted in the water as she contemplated the question. Josh tried to think about it too, but found himself rather too distracted by her bikini again.

For once, he was grateful that Iceland in February was freezing, and he was wearing several layers of clothes. Otherwise his reaction to seeing his ex-wife lounging around in the warm water in a simple black two-piece would be far greater, and far more obvious to the woman in question.

As it was, he simply adjusted his position and waited for her answer.

'I guess it depends what we want the world to think about us, after this week,' she said thoughtfully. 'Don't you think?'

'Absolutely,' Josh replied, as if he'd been reaching the same conclusion as her all along, and not thinking about how the bikini looked a lot like the sports bra and shorts she used to wear to do yoga, on the balcony outside their bedroom in LA, and the way she'd fall back into bed with him afterwards, all warm from the sun and the exercise, and pliant and flexible in his arms...

'We want them to think that we're mature, emotionally healthy professionals,' Winter went on. 'Which means being friends—or at least civil and friendly acquaintances. Yes?'

'For sure.'

Closure not closeness. That had to be his motto now. It was just hard to remember now the memories were flooding back.

'That's settled, then.' Winter smiled up at him, and he tried to shake away the images of them in bed and focus on what they'd actually agreed.

'So we act like disinterested friends in

public, polite but not close?' That he could manage.

'And then when we come back here we can, well, talk. Find that closure we apparently need.' The face Winter pulled at the word 'closure' told Josh she wasn't entirely convinced she needed it.

But he was, more and more. If the universe had given him another opportunity to spend some time with this woman, and maybe even understand exactly what he'd done wrong in their marriage—so he could get it right next time…well. He wasn't idiotic enough to turn that down.

Maybe Liam was right, and he really could find love again. The sort of love his parents had shared, that his brother and Ashley had now. True love, that was right from the start—and stayed right.

That was worth some difficult conversations. Wasn't it?

An hour or so later, skin still pink from the lagoon, Winter wound her way through the hotel corridors back to the main atrium, looking for her wayward assistant—and maybe a hot chocolate. Josh had left her to soak after their conversation, and she'd stayed in the lagoon longer than she'd meant to, lulled by the clear air, the warm water and the empty grey of the skies.

She was glad she'd come, despite her initial misgivings. Maybe Jenny was right, and some closure with Josh would be nice. But, even more than that, the chance to slow down, relax and let the water and the air chase away some of her worries—before the next round of whatever chaos came next hit—could only be good.

Winter had never been particularly good at slowing down, except when forced by circumstance. But she knew from past bitter experience that not giving her body what it needed when it needed it could never end well. So now she tried to take a break once in a while, give her physical self the time to catch up with her mile-a-minute mind.

She might not like it, but she knew now that it was necessary, if she didn't want her body to betray her again.

She came to the main atrium, with its wide open-plan space and huge glass walls, and smiled. Everything felt so…open here. As if anything was possible. She liked that.

Winter found Jenny sitting in the coffee shop area with Liam and raised her eyebrows at the sight.

'Does this place do a good hot chocolate?'

she asked as she slipped into an empty chair at their table.

'The best.' Liam flashed her a smile and started to raise his hand to a staff member, but Jenny jumped to her feet first.

'I'll get it, boss,' she said, hurrying towards the counter.

'So, how did you find your suite? Jenny said you planned to try out the private lagoon. How was it?' Liam leaned back in his chair, long legs stretched out in front of him, arms folded over his chest and a familiar knowing smirk on his lips.

Winter resisted the urge to poke him in the ribs. 'Less private than advertised.'

'Ah.' The smirk turned into a smile. 'You met your neighbour, then?'

'You mean my ex-husband? Yes.'

'And?' Liam pressed.

Winter huffed a sigh. 'And what? What do you imagine happened? We suddenly and simultaneously realised the error of our ways and fell into each other's arms?'

'A guy can dream, can't he?'

'I seriously doubt that *your* dreams involve *my* love life,' Winter said caustically.

'Okay, fine. Is the best suite in the hotel still standing, or do I need to send the builders in?' Liam asked, then lowered his voice. 'Jenny told me about the screaming.'

Winter shot a glare at her assistant, where she was waiting for hot chocolate. 'Jenny should remember the non-disclosure contract she signed.'

Liam barked a laugh. 'I expect after five years she knows you too well to think you'd ever actually sue her. Besides, the way I see it, she knows where all the bodies are buried. You need to keep her close.'

'If you mean she knows where my plane tickets and passport are, my calendar for the next three years and the phone numbers of everyone who matters to me, you're right.' Jenny was the best damn assistant in Hollywood. Everyone knew that.

Winter's eyes narrowed. Suddenly, Liam and Jenny's coffee date made a lot more sense.

'You're trying to steal her from me,' she said.

Liam threw up his hands in mock innocence. 'I swear I have no idea what you're talking about.'

'Jenny. You know she's the best in the business and you want to hire her away from me.'

The innocent look slid away, and Liam shook his head. 'I promise you I'm not. I know how important she is to you, and I wouldn't do that.'

Somehow, that wasn't as reassuring as Winter had hoped. Because if Liam wasn't talking to Jenny for a job interview, that meant... 'Did you two conspire together on this?'

Jenny, returning with the drinks, slopped a little hot chocolate over the side as she placed them on the table. 'Winter, are you getting paranoid on me? Because all I did was go fetch hot chocolate.'

'No, you didn't. You sent me out into the geothermal lagoon outside our room but didn't want to come with me, when all you've been talking about for weeks was how much you were looking forward to sinking into it. You said you wouldn't come out of the water all week. And instead I find you here, talking to *him*.'

'Hey!' Liam protested. 'I resent whatever implication your tone there was making about my character.'

Winter waved an apologetic hand in his direction. 'Oh, you know what I mean. You two set me up.' Realising she was drawing more than a little attention from the group sitting at the next table, she lowered her voice as she accused Jenny, 'You knew Josh was staying next door. Didn't you?'

Jenny wiggled uncomfortably on her chair, then looked at Liam and shrugged. 'I told you I won't lie to her.' She turned back to Winter. 'I swear I didn't know until we got here this afternoon. Liam told me when he was showing me to our room.'

'So this is all your cunning plan, then,' Winter said to Liam. 'Dare I ask what you were hoping to achieve from this?'

A shadow fell across the table, and suddenly the fourth chair was being pulled out and Josh was sitting on it, claiming the second hot chocolate Jenny had brought but hadn't touched. This was definitely feeling more like a conspiracy than ever.

She wondered if she could blame the conspiracy for the warm feeling that started in her chest as she looked at her ex-husband, sitting at her side, looking for all the world as if the last five years had just been a nightmare she was now waking up from.

Winter looked away. Because it hadn't been a nightmare. Those five years had happened, and she had survived, and there was no way she could risk going backwards again now. Not when she'd worked so hard to get to where she was.

'Thanks for this, Jenny,' Josh said with a friendly smile. 'Sorry, got caught by a couple of autograph-hunters—I'd keep your head down, Winter, or they'll be after the full set.'

Winter scowled. Because, of course, people were only interested in her in relation to her ex-husband. As always. At least his comment was a timely reminder of one of the many reasons it was a good thing they were no longer together.

I'm my own person now. I went through hell to get there, and I'm not going back.

'Now, where were we?' Josh said lightly. 'Ah, yes. Liam. What exactly *were* you hoping to achieve by putting Winter and me in adjoining rooms?' He sipped his hot chocolate, raising his eyebrows over the rim of the mug, looking for all the world as if he was just asking about the weather, or what was for dinner.

Winter hid a smile as Liam squirmed a little under that friendly but unflinching gaze.

'I guess I just hoped the two of you would… find a way to be friends again,' he said eventually. 'I don't have many friends these days, you might have noticed. And with you two each pretending the other doesn't exist, it makes birthday parties and the like a tad difficult.'

Winter and Josh exchanged a quick glance. Liam had been through a lot these past few years, as much as they had. Even if they hadn't already decided to try to find some closure on the two of them, Winter knew that Liam's casual comment about birthday parties—and all the loss and pain she could hear beneath his words—would have convinced her.

'We are,' she said softly. 'Trying the friends thing, I mean.'

'Really?' Liam sat up straight with obvious surprise. '*Really*, really?'

Beside her, Josh rolled his eyes and slapped his friend lightly on the shoulder. 'Really, *really*, really, you idiot. Your plan worked. Soon you can throw all the birthday parties you want.'

Liam's smile turned devious. 'Only if Jenny comes too. Winter gave me the wonderful idea of trying to steal her away into my employ, but I think I'm going to need more than one week to manage that, so—'

'Hey!' Now it was Winter's turn to reach across and bat his other shoulder with the back of her hand, although she couldn't stop herself grinning. 'That was not an invitation.'

'No, those will need to have balloons on them,' Liam said, clearly delighting in the nonsense. 'Jenny, maybe you can help me with those?'

Jenny raised her eyebrows at him. 'You'd have to make it worth my while.'

'Ah, a woman who knows her worth. That's my kind of girl.'

As Liam leant across the table towards her assistant to begin his ridiculous negotiation over party invites for a birthday that Winter happened to know was at least six months away, she glanced over at Josh and found him already watching her, a soft smile on his face.

She returned it and watched his widen—then looked away fast as her treacherous heart skipped a beat.

This was how it had started last time. Secret smiles and knowing looks. Moments where the world disappeared and it was only them left in the universe.

Her heart skipping whenever he smiled at her.

Josh had told the world that when he'd met her gaze across that crowded film set, the day they'd met, he'd known that he was going to marry her. Nobody had asked Winter what she'd thought in that moment, but if they had she'd have told them.

She'd known that the man who looked at her that way, who smiled and made her heart skip, was the sort of man who could change the direction of her life.

She just hadn't known if that change would be for good or for bad. But she'd been young and hopeful, and she'd taken that risk.

Now, seeing that same smile, she knew she couldn't take that chance again. Not for anything.

Not when it had almost destroyed everything about her last time.

Friends. She could do friends. It was her suggestion, for heaven's sake.

But *just* friends.

Yes. This was fine. This was going to be fine. Probably not a disaster at all.

She chanced another look, and Josh flashed that smile her way again, causing her certainty on that point to waver.

Probably fine, she reminded herself. *Just as long as I avoid that smile and don't throw myself at him over the next week, things will be absolutely, probably, fine. Probably.*

CHAPTER FIVE

LIAM HAD PLANNED a full programme of activities for the week, designed to show off the hotel and the surrounding area in their best possible light. Which was why Josh found himself, the following morning, queuing at the breakfast buffet far earlier than seemed reasonable, dressed in several more layers of clothing than he'd have needed if he'd just stayed in LA like a sensible person.

Outside the wide windows the sun wasn't even up yet, although Josh guessed that had more to do with the northern location than the actual hour. Still, from the yawns and demands for coffee, he suspected he wasn't the only one resenting the early start.

Their host, meanwhile, seemed in high spirits as he made his way around the breakfast room, with its glorious views over towards the icy mountains, clapping people on the back and making jokes. Shaking his head at his friend, Josh was about to go find a secluded table where he might escape Liam's early morning exuberance, when he spotted a familiar dark head of hair.

Winter. She was dressed like everyone else, in warm layers, ready for the day's adventures, and he could see a scarf and hat poking out of the bag slung over her shoulder. Josh hesitated. They hadn't spoken much after the hot chocolate with Liam and Jenny the day before, and when he'd headed out to enjoy the lagoon that evening she hadn't joined him. But if they were going to be friends—or even just act that way in public—shouldn't he ask her to join him now?

From the look on her face, he wasn't sure if the overture would be appreciated. So he watched a little longer instead.

Jenny stood beside her, yawning, her blonde hair twisted up into plaits on the back of her head. But while she had a full plate of food, Winter's remained empty. As she turned her head away from the buffet, he could make out the strain around her eyes, and the forced smile on her lips.

He let his gaze scan back over the breakfast buffet, and felt his breath catch as he hit on a probable reason for her discomfort.

Smoked fish.

Five years hadn't taken away the memories, it seemed. Even the small ones.

Decision made, he dashed forward, taking Jenny's arm and smiling broadly. 'Ladies! Just the breakfast companions I was waiting for. I've secured the *perfect* table, just over there.' He pointed vaguely at the last remaining window table and hoped no one else could steal it before they got there. 'Why don't you go sit down while I finish getting breakfast for us?'

Jenny was frowning at him in confusion. 'But Winter hasn't—'

'Don't worry!' he said, probably too loud. 'Leave it to me.'

'Come on, Jenny,' Winter said softly, and the two of them headed for the table he'd indicated.

Letting out a relieved breath, Josh quickly filled two plates with pastries, dark rye bread, jam and other inoffensive morning foods— choosing to leave most of the Icelandic specialities alone for now. While he'd be happy to try the *skyr*—a thick yogurt cheese—another time, he didn't want to tempt fate with Winter's stomach. And he couldn't remember ever seeing her eat oatmeal in the mornings, so he left the *hafragrautur* for now too.

The fish-based breakfast items were definitely off the menu.

Before he carried the plates over to the table, though, he collared one of the hotel staff and put in a special request—one he hoped they'd be able to fulfil before they left for the day's adventures. Then he headed over to join Winter and Jenny. Except Jenny had moved away to take a phone call, leaving him alone at the table with his ex-wife.

'How did you know?' Winter asked, looking down at her plate of bland, easy to eat foods.

Josh huffed a laugh. 'Trust me. You throwing up all down my tux at that charity ball is the sort of thing that stays with a man. It was the smoked fish again, right?'

She nodded. 'I can't believe it still bothers me. But even now, after all these years, my stomach still turns when I smell it.'

That night had been their first clue, Josh remembered, before the pregnancy test the next day had confirmed it. Winter had been feeling absolutely fine—maybe a little tired, but that wasn't unusual given how hard she'd been working. He'd pushed her to rest a little more, but she'd persuaded him to join her for a lie down, and neither of them had really rested very much after that.

They'd almost been late for the charity ball they'd agreed to attend, Winter still tying his bow tie in the cab there, both of them giggling at the reason for their lateness. Then, an hour or so later, after welcome drinks, the waiting staff had put a plate of smoked fish starters on the table in front of Winter, she'd taken one breath, turned to him and vomited. They'd had to reassure everyone else in the room that it wasn't a reaction to the food… but they hadn't known for sure what it was until she took the test.

But that night…that had been the start of everything, in his mind. The moment when the world had changed and the wonderful fairy tale he'd been living in had started to fracture. That afternoon in bed the last time anything had felt truly normal between them. God, he missed that.

'I'm sorry,' he said. She looked at him with surprise, and he wondered if maybe she felt that same longing for how things had been that he did. 'That it didn't go away, I mean.'

Except that wasn't really all he meant. He was sorry for so many things, he didn't think he'd ever be able to make up for them all. Not if he brought her breakfast every day for the rest of her life. Which she'd pretty much turned down the day she'd walked out on their marriage.

I'm sorry for everything I did that made you leave. Or everything I couldn't do. I'm sorry that you couldn't talk to me about any of it. That I couldn't fix it for you.

'Yeah,' she said. 'Me too.'

Before they could say anything else, Jenny returned, dropping into her seat, already talking a mile a minute to Winter about whoever had been on the other end of the call. Josh turned his attention to his own plate of food, and only smiled when the hotel worker he'd asked for a favour slipped a small packet into his hand when Liam gathered them all in the foyer, ready to leave on the day's adventure.

He couldn't fix things then. But maybe he could remind her that he cared.

As a friend, of course.

'Do you think we'll actually see some whales?' Jenny asked as they boarded the boat Liam had hired for them for the day.

'I think that's kind of the point of a whale-watching trip.' Winter eyed the boat with some trepidation. Her stomach was still a little unsure about everything after her encounter with the fish plates at breakfast, and she wasn't convinced that spending several hours out on the rolling waves was going to improve matters any.

'Yeah, but whales are freedom-loving creatures,' Jenny went on. 'I mean, how can anyone be sure exactly where they're going to be today?'

The boat was leaving from Reykjavik's Old Harbour, and Winter could see a number of other whale-watching tour boats being offered, although Liam had booked one out solely for their use.

She pointed to a poster. 'They seem to reckon a ninety-nine percent chance of seeing *something*.'

Jenny raised her eyebrows, arms folded across her chest with either scepticism or cold, it was hard to tell. 'I'll believe it when I see it.'

'It *is* a little harder to find them at this time of year.' Appearing behind them, Liam slung an arm over each of their shoulders as he guided them further onto the boat. 'But I'm assured of at least one small minke whale, and maybe a few harbour porpoises. Plus we get to enjoy all this fantastic scenery. Volcanoes to the south, maybe even a glimpse of the Snæfellsjökull Glacier if we head north.'

Winter leaned against the rail around the edge of the boat, the chill of it still biting through all the layers of clothes she'd put on. 'Are we going to freeze to death out there? Because I feel that wouldn't look good in your promotional brochure.'

Liam laughed. 'There are warm overalls over there that you can put on if you need.' He gestured towards the centre of the boat, where a staff member was handing out padded clothing. 'And if that isn't enough, the cabin at the centre there is heated too, so you can head inside to warm up. Just don't blame me if you miss a whale!'

With a final clap on their shoulders, he headed off to check on his other guests, and Winter and Jenny, in unspoken agreement, moved to grab some of the padded overalls.

Winter paused for a second when she realised Josh was already there. The conversation they'd had at breakfast, and all the words they hadn't said, weighed as heavily in her stomach as the pastries she was wishing she hadn't eaten. Neither of them had even said the word 'pregnant' or talked about—she swallowed before finishing the thought—the baby she'd lost. But, all the same, she knew it was the only thing she'd think about for the rest of the day.

Not that *that* was so unusual. There hadn't been a day in five years where she hadn't thought about it. Hadn't hated herself for not being enough, hated her body for letting her down.

A miscarriage sounded like such a small thing. Like a misstep, or at worse a mistake.

But it had shaped Winter's entire life ever since.

Jenny handed her a pair of overalls and Winter made herself step forward and stay in the present, not the past. Iceland in winter was nothing to be joking about and she wanted to be properly prepared.

Beside her, Josh yanked his overalls up over his shoulders and replaced his thick coat over the top, then fished something out of his pocket to hand to her. 'Just in case,' he said, and gave her a wink as he closed her fingers around a small packet before turning and walking away.

'What's that?' Jenny asked, watching her curiously.

Winter unfurled her fingers to find a small packet of ginger chews inside. 'Where on earth did he get these?'

'Ooh, are those for seasickness?' One of the influencer girls had appeared at Winter's side and was eyeing them covetously. 'Can I get one? I'm desperate to see the whales, but

I just know my stomach's going to hate those waves.'

They all looked out at the choppy waters unhappily. 'Absolutely,' Winter said, and started handing them around.

By the time they were out at sea, the coastline around Reykjavik harbour retreating by the second, half of Winter's ginger chews were gone, but she hoped she was starting to find her sea legs. Maybe it was the brisk chill of the salty air against her face, or the excitement of watching for sea creatures, or just being somewhere so unlike anywhere she'd seen before. Whatever it was, it seemed enough to distract her from her rolling stomach— and even a little from the conversation over breakfast, and the memories it had stirred up.

They'd seen some seabirds circling, and Winter was still hoping for puffins when they came further in against the coast, but so far the dolphins and whales had eluded them. Jenny was looking increasingly sceptical about the whole venture, even after Liam's reassurances that the crew would have already been out to sea even earlier that morning, to discover where the whales were hiding today.

'It's pretty incredible here, isn't it?' Josh leaned against the railings beside her, looking out to sea the same way she was. He raised a hand to point northwards. 'Somewhere up there is some ice-topped mountain that Jules Verne said was the entrance to the inside of the planet.'

'*Journey to the Centre of the Earth*,' Winter murmured. 'Weren't you up for a part in a remake of that once?'

'Probably.'

They stood in companionable silence, staring out at the water for a long moment, until Josh said, 'It's not too awful, this friendship thing, is it?'

Hearing the hope in his voice, Winter smiled down at the water and thought about breakfast pastries and ginger chews. None of it erased all those painful memories, or even started to make up for them. But Josh knew her in a way that no one else in the world did. Had lived some of her very worst moments with her.

Having him back in her life, in some small way…it made her feel more like herself, somehow. Or, maybe, the woman she used to be.

But I decided I didn't want to be her any more. Didn't I?

Could there be a way to reclaim the parts of herself she'd liked back then, and add them to the woman she'd become? It was something to think about, anyway.

'Do I take this ominous silence as an *Actually, Joshua, it's horrible and I just don't know how to tell you*?'

She huffed a laugh. 'No. I was just…thinking. That maybe Liam was right, and friendship might be good for us.'

'God, don't tell him that,' Josh joked. 'His smugness will know no bounds.'

Suddenly a call went up from the raised platform above the cabin, and the boat buzzed with excitement as everyone hurried to the starboard side of the vessel.

'What is it?' Winter asked, as they caught up to Liam and Jenny.

'A whale, of course! A minke, they think,' Liam said. 'Someone saw the spray of water from a blowhole so now we just wait and—ah!'

She saw it, then. The sleek, shining skin of a minke whale, water sluicing off it as it broke the surface, just a short way from their boat. Around her, she heard gasps and camera shutters on phones, but Winter just watched and let the moment fill her with wonder, stretching the seconds out as the whale crested and dived again, sending a spray of icy water towards the boat.

It was moments like this that had got her through the months and years after the miscarriage, and the collapse of her marriage. Small moments of wonder that made the world feel bright again, just for a little while. That gave hope.

It wasn't until the creature had disappeared fully under the waves that she realised she was holding Josh's hand. Worse, she didn't know if she'd grabbed him, or he'd grabbed her.

Winter had avoided him for the rest of the boat trip, staying far on the other side of the crowd as they'd spotted a pod of dolphins on their way back to shore. Josh tried not to take it personally. After all, they'd only just agreed to try friendship, and already the memories and emotions that had brought up had been intense. And if he was feeling that, he could only imagine how much worse it was for her.

In her eyes on the boat he'd seen a glimpse of the fractured woman she'd been after she lost their baby. The one he'd left behind when he'd gone to work on his latest movie—and returned two months later to find her gone.

This time, he wouldn't leave, not until they'd talked about everything that had happened between them—everything neither of them had felt able to discuss at the time.

But he would give her space. He ordered room service for dinner, and later heard her leaving for the restaurant with Jenny. So once he'd finished eating, he decided to take advantage of her absence and enjoy that private geothermal lagoon he'd been promised.

The evening air bit at his skin as he stepped outside in his swimming gear, towel draped over his arm, regretting leaving behind the fluffy bathrobe that came with the room. Still, it was only a few steps before he was sinking into the naturally warmed waters of the lagoon, the rocks smooth against his spine.

Josh let his head fall back until he was staring up at the night sky. It wasn't late, not by anyone's standards, but darkness dropped early and suddenly so far north. The last twenty-four hours had been...overwhelming, and to sit there in the dark and the silence was soothing.

He'd taken his watch off, and his phone was somewhere inside, so he didn't know how long he'd been soaking there when he heard the glass doors behind him slide open. The water swirling around him, he turned to fold his arms over the rocks at the edge of the pool and rested his chin on them.

Winter stepped out onto the decking, wrapped in a fluffy bathrobe just like the one he'd neglected, and carrying two white mugs.

'Hot chocolate,' she said, as if it were perfectly normal for her to be bringing him hot drinks late at night.

'I can get out, if you want?' The thought of abandoning the warmth of the water for the bitter air he could already feel, sharp against his bare back, was not a nice one. But he had been hogging the lagoon all evening. 'I've probably been in here long enough, anyway.'

After placing the two mugs on the decking, within arm's reach of the lagoon, Winter let the bathrobe fall from her shoulders, revealing a different swimsuit from yesterday's. This one was red, had only one shoulder strap, and a cut-out below it that showcased her trim waist. It also did things to Josh's blood that even the warmth of the geothermal springs couldn't match.

Closure not closeness, he reminded his rebellious body. It didn't listen.

'It's fine.' She slid into the water, a little way apart from him. 'It's plenty big enough, anyway.'

That much was definitely true. When Liam had first tried to sell him on this trip with the promise of a private lagoon, Josh had assumed he was just talking up what was basically a hot tub. But this pool was something else entirely. Large enough for a football team, it seemed positively decadent to have it to share between just the two of them—and Jenny, he supposed, although she seemed to have made herself scarce again.

Because of the way the rooms were angled, to one side at the back of the hotel, and with a rocky barrier between them and the suites around the next corner, lying submerged in the water together they could have been the last two people left on earth.

Josh reached behind him for his hot chocolate and took a sip. Already, the freezing air had cooled it to a comfortable drinking temperature.

'Is it okay?' Winter asked from across the pool. 'I could have made coffee, I suppose. Or found some wine, or something. But Jenny brought you a hot chocolate yesterday, so—'

'It's perfect,' he said, cutting her off. 'Thank you.'

'Okay. Good.'

'I mean, not as good as the stuff you used to make after a late-night shoot. You remember? With the cream and the marshmallows and the nutmeg grated on top?' Sometimes, he still dreamt about those hot chocolates.

Especially after a really long night filming, when he started hallucinating his bed. The thought of Winter at home waiting for him, with one of her hot chocolates ready, had been the only thing to sustain him some nights.

'I remember,' she murmured, and they both lapsed back into silence.

These days, Josh reflected, he had to make do with hotel room service. And he was more likely to call for a whisky than a hot chocolate.

He took another sip and savoured the taste. He couldn't imagine he'd be experiencing it again after this week, however well their plan for friendship and closure worked. There was something intimate about late night drinks like this.

Maybe that was what he had missed most of all. Not the cream, or the marshmallows, or the nutmeg. Just coming home to Winter—or having her come home to him.

And that was something he couldn't get back. He'd failed at that once already. They'd tried, and they knew it didn't work between them. Better to learn the lessons now and try again with someone new.

Because losing Winter twice? No man could survive that.

'Thank you,' she said, her voice so quiet he

had to strain to hear it. 'For breakfast and for the ginger chews. That's why…why I brought the hot chocolate. To say thank you.'

'You're welcome.' It was such a small thing to thank him for. Nowhere near as much as he owed her.

He hadn't been able to fix all the things that had been wrong between them, in the end. Or the things that came from outside their control to destroy them.

He hadn't been able to save their baby.

Ginger chews were nothing.

'So,' he said, after he'd finished his hot chocolate. 'I figure we're getting pretty good at the friendship thing, right?'

Winter nodded. 'Which brings us to the second part of the plan. Closure.'

They hadn't admitted that part to Liam or Jenny, by mutual—if unarticulated—agreement. This part, this was just for them. To help them move on.

'How do we do that, exactly?'

Taking a deep breath, Winter placed her own mug beside his on the decking, and turned to face him, her eyes dark and serious under the subdued and unobtrusive lighting placed around the decking, and the pale light of the moon from overhead. 'I've been thinking about that. And I've got one idea.'

There was something in her voice. A warning, perhaps. Or maybe just a reluctance. Either way, Josh got the impression that whatever this idea was, he wasn't going to like it very much.

But it wasn't as if he had any better notions about how to find closure on their marriage. If he had, he'd have used them already, and let his failures go. It was this or nothing.

Josh braced himself against the rocks of the pool. 'Tell me.'

CHAPTER SIX

WINTER WAS PRETTY sure that this was a terrible idea. Why else had she been putting it off? Going for dinner with Jenny, then making hot chocolate, letting him talk about old times and night shoots?

She'd been half hoping that he'd have some ideas of his own. Or maybe decided to pack the whole thing in and head back to LA and leave her to her lagoon in peace.

But no. He sat there, half naked and gorgeous and distracting in the moonlight, and said, '*Tell me.*'

So she did.

'I think…there was a lot we left unsaid at the end. And I know a lot of that was my fault for the way I left. But I feel like…like the words are still sitting inside us, taking up space. And maybe we need to get them out.' She took a breath. 'So my suggestion is that we share a secret, each night we're here.'

'Get them all out,' Josh said contemplatively. 'Let them all go.'

'Exactly.' She was glad he'd got it so easily. She hadn't been sure.

When they'd first met, they'd talked all night sometimes. Genuinely forgotten to go to sleep because they were so wrapped up in hearing each other's thoughts on the world. But it seemed to Winter now that all that talking had been in the abstract, rather than anything useful.

Dreams for the future, favourite books, where they'd love to travel. Stories about growing up, from their fledgling careers, about family and friends. All important things to share.

But when it came to the problems that arose between them, she'd found herself suddenly mute. Weighed down by the romance of the fairy tale everyone told about them, admitting things weren't perfect had seemed impossible—especially when, for Josh, they obviously were. He loved to talk about 'his wife' or to find another film for them to appear in together, or to show up on those red carpets with her on his arm.

And she'd loved it too, to start with. Until the feeling that the person she was underneath all the trappings of their fame and their story was starting to blur, to disappear at the edges beneath the myth of who people said she was.

She'd tried to explain it to Josh once, but the lack of comprehension on his face told her he couldn't feel the same. Couldn't understand how she felt.

Then she'd fallen pregnant, and he'd been away filming, and the silence had gaped wide, seeming to push them further and further apart.

It was too late now to draw them back together, but having those hard conversations they'd avoided for so long might help with the closure they both so obviously needed.

'So. Do you want to go first?' The hope was clear in his voice.

'Not really,' she admitted. 'But I will.'

She should have planned this better. She hadn't thought beyond getting him to agree to her plan, to what secret she'd actually share first. There were so many of them swirling around her head, she didn't know where to start.

She sucked in a deep breath and decided to start small. 'The ginger chews, and breakfast.'

Josh frowned and shifted closer towards her under the water. 'What about them? They didn't really help? I could try something else—'

She cut him off with a shake of her head. 'They did help. And I appreciated both gestures—really I did. Just like I appreciated all the things you did to try and help me five years ago.'

The memories came rolling back in, the way she'd known they would. Because that incident Josh had joked about, her throwing up on his tux at that charity dinner, had only been the start.

She'd heard about morning sickness before, even expected it when she realised she was pregnant. But she'd never been prepared for what followed over the next few months.

It wasn't just that the sickness wasn't constrained to one part of the day or night. Or that foods she'd previously loved suddenly turned her stomach. She could have lived without coffee—quite happily, given the queasy feeling that came over her at the smell.

All of that was awful—but she would have suffered it stoically for her baby. Of course she would.

Josh had been on hand, when he could be, bringing her anything she thought she might be able to stomach that day, or making sure she napped and didn't worry about other things. And when he'd been away, filming or rehearsing, he'd sent constant emails and texts with links to articles and folk remedies. He'd shipped bottles of useless tablets and tonics directly to her, along with the endless packets of ginger chews which, at least, helped dim the nausea for the brief time she was chewing them.

None of it had helped for long.

The real problems had started when she'd been unable to keep any food down—even those damn ginger chews. Then it had progressed to any liquids. To even the feel of water touching her throat leaving her vomiting helplessly again.

Her doctors had been concerned. Samples taken, levels tested, and a diagnosis of *hyperemesis gravidarum* given. There were tablets to try, and an overnight stay in hospital to rehydrate her more than once.

Still none of it lasted long, and all the doctors could suggest was that she rest and try to get through it.

And still Josh kept sending new things to try, new ways to fix her.

And *that,* she'd realised later, was the problem with the ginger chews. Much later, as it happened—once the sickness was over, and the grieving that had followed had dulled a little too. Once she was miles away from her ex-husband, and her thoughts had started to make sense to her again.

'So? What was the secret about the ginger chews?' Josh asked, still looking baffled.

Winter tried to find the right words. She didn't want to sound ungrateful, or uncaring. And she didn't really want to make him feel bad for trying to do the right thing. But they'd agreed to share the secrets that had ended their marriage and, for her, this was where that ending had started.

'When I was so sick... I know you were trying to help me, and I appreciated that even then. But it also made me feel like, well, like you were trying to fix me. Like I was so broken you had to find a fast solution so I could be myself again, the woman you loved, that you'd married. So I could get back to my role in our story. And I knew then, even in my bones, that I'd never be that woman again.' She looked down at her moonlit reflection in the water and thought she could almost see the weight of the secret rising from it, with the steam from the geothermal lagoon. 'You were trying to fix me, and all I wanted was to see you. To have you with me. For you to *listen* to me, and empathise, without trying to make it all go away. Because then, when it did—'

She broke off, unable to find any words for that part. For when she'd lost that longed-for baby who had already made life so hard but was also already so loved. Her miscarriage had been a quirk of fate, she was assured by everyone from friends and family to medical professionals. She mustn't blame herself, there was nothing she could have done.

But she *had* blamed herself. Because she was the one who'd got out of bed, felt dizzy and fallen on the stairs. She was the one whose body hadn't been able to handle the trauma of the pregnancy and the fall. The one who had failed at motherhood before she'd even had the chance to try.

And worse still was the fear that followed. That Josh might be glad, because he thought he could have the old Winter back, even though she no longer existed.

More terrifying even was the idea that he might want to try again.

She knew Josh, knew he wanted the picket fence and two-point-four kids. And when she'd married him, she had too. But now she knew that was beyond her capabilities— physical, mental or emotional.

She could not risk getting pregnant again.

Not after the fear and the pain and the loss of last time.

And that was when she'd known she had to move on and let him find that with someone else.

Across the pool, Josh looked poleaxed by her words, his mouth slightly open, his knuckles white as he clenched his fist against the decking. 'Winter. I—'

But she couldn't hear it. She couldn't bear it.

Water sluicing down her body, she hurriedly climbed out from the lagoon, grabbing blindly for her robe as she rushed towards her room.

That was all the secrets she could take for one night.

Josh didn't sleep. He dozed, but only to dream of those horrific days trying to care for Winter from thousands of miles away, seeing only her drawn and exhausted face on the other end of a phone screen.

Even when he woke, things weren't much better. Her pale face in the moonlight as she'd described how she'd felt during that time haunted him just as much.

I need to talk to her.

He had so many things still to say. To

explain—if not excuse. To try and understand better what she'd been through. Because if he hadn't seen this—how his trying to fix things was only making her feel more broken—what else had he missed? How else had he screwed up without even knowing?

He'd thought she blamed him for not being there, but now he wondered how much more there was behind it. And he needed to know.

But he didn't imagine she'd appreciate him breaking into her room at three in the morning to discuss the matter further, so instead he turned his pillow over, settled down and tried to sleep.

He failed.

By the time seven a.m. rolled around and breakfast was being served in the restaurant, he'd given up. To his surprise, Liam was already in the restaurant with a cup of coffee and a plate of food, so he joined him to find out his fate for the day.

'What is it today?' Josh slipped into the seat opposite his friend, his own cup of—very strong—coffee in hand. 'I mean, how are you going to top whale-watching? Is it a hike up a glacier? A trip to a volcano? Waterfalls? Ice caves? What?' Something active. Something to keep his body busy and his mind occupied with everything around him. That was what he needed today—a distraction. At least until Winter was ready to talk to him again.

Liam tutted at him over the rim of his coffee cup. 'Nothing so dramatic. Today, all my guests will be at their leisure to enjoy the incredible spa facilities here at the Ice House Hotel. In fact, I took the liberty of drawing up a schedule for you.' He fished a polished piece of card from the folder on the table, neatly printed with a list of treatments and timings for him to use the sauna, steam rooms and other spa facilities.

'I have to do all of this?' Josh asked, scanning down the list. 'It looks...excessive.'

'You've been working hard, these past few years,' Liam said blandly. 'You could do with a proper relaxing break.'

The schedule looked more like a route march through organised relaxation to Josh, but he didn't mention that to his friend. Maybe he could opt out when he got bored.

He stayed and shot the breeze with Liam over breakfast until his friend needed to get to work. Josh poured himself another coffee, reclaimed his table and watched the other guests filter down for their own morning meal.

Except two. There was no sign of Winter, or Jenny.

With a sigh, Josh resigned himself to the idea that they must have asked for room service that morning. And he couldn't imagine that his ex-wife would be wandering out to the geothermal lagoon anytime soon, not after last night. Which meant if he wanted to talk to her, he needed to stick to Liam's schedule for the day and hope that his and Winter's coincided.

Knowing Liam, he suspected they would.

Thirty minutes later, Josh showed up as instructed at the entrance to the spa area of the hotel. Here, the glass walls and bright openness gave way to more warmth and wooden touches, leading him down a cocooning hallway to the reception desk.

He handed the smiling woman behind the desk his card, and was led to a locker room where he could change and prepare himself. Then he made his way to what was called the Lupina Suite. 'All our treatment rooms are named after native wildflowers,' his guide explained. 'Here you are. Enjoy your massage!' The door swung shut behind him, and he was committed to his fate.

Josh had experienced plenty of sports massages in his time, but he suspected this would be something different. A feeling that was confirmed by the soft panpipe music and natural world sounds being piped into the room, the dim, womb-like lighting and the fact that his ex-wife was sitting on one of the two massage tables in the space.

'Liam booked us a couples massage,' she said, holding the fluffy robe she wore a little tighter around her body, her fingers clenched around the fabric at her throat.

'Of course he did.'

At least they weren't alone in the room. Within moments, they'd been joined by their masseuses and were both lying on their fronts on their tables, towels just about covering their modesty.

Josh made a point of not peeking at Winter's table as she lay there. No point in making this any more awkward than it already was. But just knowing she was there, practically naked, covered in massage oil, just a few feet away…he had to admit it was bringing up memories she'd probably rather he wasn't thinking about right then.

His lack of sleep caught up with him on the table, though. As the talented and well-trained masseur worked his hands over his back, Josh felt some of the tension he'd been storing in his muscles all week start to dissipate. He couldn't forget the secrets Winter had shared the night before, but he could at least put them in the context of five years ago, and deal with them with a more distant eye.

He'd dozed off by the time his massage was finished and only realised the masseuses had left the room when Winter said, 'Apparently we're to lie here and relax for fifteen minutes before we get up.'

'When did they say that?' He hadn't seen it on the schedule.

'When you fell asleep.'

'I didn't—'

'I know your sleeping breathing, Josh,' she countered. 'You were dead to the world.'

He sighed into the towel pillow beneath his head. 'I didn't sleep well last night.'

Her breath hitched at that, before she said, 'Neither did I.'

For a moment the only sound between them was the waves crashing against the sand being piped through the sound system, backed by the odd gull, far away, and the start of another panpipe refrain.

Then they both spoke at once.

'I didn't mean to—' Winter started.

'I need to say—' Josh stopped and lifted his head enough to smile at her across the room. She rested with her head on one side, still lying on her front, looking back at him with wide eyes. The towel that covered her left her calves, her shoulders and her upper back bare, and they all gleamed with oil in the dim light.

God, I want to touch her.

There was so much he still didn't understand about how things had ended between them—more than he'd ever realised he didn't know. But he had to remember the reasons for finding out—to avoid making the same mistakes again. So he could move on and find love with someone who didn't break a little every time she looked at him. Whose presence didn't remind him of all his screwups.

Someone he could get things right with from the start.

He forced himself to swallow and focus on the conversation at hand. 'I need to say I'm sorry,' he said when it became clear she was waiting for him to speak first. 'I'm so sorry. Everything you said last night... I wasn't trying to *fix* you, because you never needed fixing. But I can understand why you felt that way and I'm sorry, so sorry, I couldn't be what you needed then.'

She dipped her chin, an accepting nod that looked strange in her lying position. 'What *were* you trying to do?'

Taking care to keep his towel in place, Josh turned on his side to face her as he thought about his answer. 'I guess I was trying to...be there, even when I wasn't. You were so miserable, and so ill, and I knew that there was nothing I could do to make it better, but that didn't make me stop trying. Because...'

'Because?' she prompted.

He sighed. 'Because I knew it was my fault. And I felt guilty as hell about that.'

Winter turned towards him in surprise, only remembering at the last minute to grab her towel to make sure it came with her.

'You thought my sickness was *your* fault?' All these years, she'd thought he'd been frustrated by her illness, disappointed by her inability to do pregnancy right, the same way she had. She'd always imagined, when she'd thought about it at all, being on Josh's arm at a premiere in a cute as hell maternity cocktail dress and improbably high heels, glowing for the cameras. She'd assumed that was what *he'd* imagined too.

Not her stuck in bed and stinking of sick.

Not losing the baby anyway, after everything she'd been through.

'I thought *all* of it was my fault,' Josh admitted. 'I still do. If I'd been more careful, you wouldn't have got pregnant then—I mean, it's not like we planned it, right? Because if we had, I'd have made sure I'd have been around more for when you needed me. But instead I was stuck filming on the other side of the world and you were too tired to even talk to me most nights, if our time zones even aligned, and all I could do was send you things to show that I was always, always thinking of you, even when I wasn't there with you.'

His words came out in a rush and she could hear the sincerity in them, could hear how badly he'd wanted to be there for her. How he, like she had been, had only been doing his best in a bad situation.

'I knew that,' she whispered. 'Deep down, I knew that you were trying. That we both were. But...those were such dark days. And I let that darkness overtake me sometimes.'

Josh's response was tentative. 'Like when... when we lost the baby.'

We. She'd never really thought of it as something that had happened to them as a couple, Winter realised. Only something *she* had done. *She* had lost their baby. She'd acknowledged the loss Josh felt, but still felt strangely separate from it.

'I blamed myself for that,' she admitted. 'Still do, most days. But back then... I thought that I'd spent so long wishing the sickness would go away that I'd made it happen somehow.' Because there were moments in that time, when the world wouldn't stop spinning, or when she couldn't lift her head without vomiting, that she'd have done almost *anything* to make it stop.

'No.' Josh reached out across the divide between their massage tables and grabbed her hand, squeezing it tight. 'I never thought it was your fault. Not for a moment. If anything, I blamed myself for not being there.'

The doctors at the start had tried to cheer her up, to tell her that the constant sickness was a *good* sign, that it meant a healthy baby.

Turned out they'd been wrong about that too.

For a long moment they lay there, hands clasped tight together. Winter gazed into his eyes and wondered how many other things they'd each been wrong about. That they'd blamed themselves for—and assumed the other blamed them for too.

Part of her wished they'd been able to talk like this back then, but a larger part knew that it was only the time and distance they now had between them and the events that made that possible. She was still too lost in the person the world wanted her to be, her real self shadowed by the stories the gossip websites told about her. The fairy tale romance they'd created, that had destroyed the very real love they'd shared in the end.

The woman she'd been then couldn't have managed this conversation. She was a little proud that she had now. That she'd rebuilt herself as a whole, real person again—as who she was, not who the world wanted to see. That had taken work.

But she didn't want to dwell either. She was about the future these days, not the past. They'd agreed to find closure this week, but also—she hoped—friendship. Time to get back to the more fun one of those.

'That's got to be our fifteen minutes, don't you think?' she said with an only slightly watery smile.

'Probably.' Josh gave her hand one last squeeze, then released it. 'So, what do we do now?'

Winter sat up, clasping the towel to her front. 'Why, Mr Abraham. Have you really never been on a spa day with a friend before?' She grinned, forcing a lighter tone to show him that it was okay for them to move on from the emotional conversation of earlier.

'Not exactly.'

Josh swung his legs around to sit on the

edge of the table, and Winter pointedly did not look at how much skin he showed when his towel slipped. Even with it draped across his lap to protect his modesty, his bare chest—more muscled than she remembered, probably for his latest role—was distracting enough.

Friends. That's all.

'So, you'll have to be my guide. What do we do on a friends spa day?'

She grinned, glad he'd gone with her attempt to change the mood. Too much more serious conversation and she'd have been in a ball in the corner of the sauna.

'Well, first off, we need to go try out those heated stone recliners I saw outside, because they look amazing. And if we're lucky someone might bring us a glass of something cold and bubbly while we're there.'

'That does sound good,' Josh admitted. 'What else?'

'Basically, spa days are for sitting around gossiping, drinking champagne, enjoying the steam rooms, getting our nails done and generally relaxing,' Winter said with a shrug. 'Oh, and daring each other to jump in the ice pool, of course. But, most of all, definitely gossiping.'

He raised his eyebrows at her. 'Gossiping? Really?'

'Absolutely,' Winter said firmly. 'We've got five years of news to catch up on, remember?' And now she'd got the worst of her secrets out of the way, she wanted to hear it all.

CHAPTER SEVEN

JOSH DREW THE line at getting his toenails painted pink, but he sat alongside Winter while she had hers done, and enjoyed a foot massage from another of Liam's very competent staff members. Winter's manicurist kept shooting glances between the two of them, although if she recognised them she made no comment on the two of them being there together.

Of course she didn't need to, because soon enough another trio of guests arrived for their appointment—three of Liam's influencers he was trying to seduce to the way of Iceland—and they had enough to say for everybody.

'So, are you two...you know?' One of the women—Josh thought she might be called Skylar, but he wasn't sure—waved a hand between them in a meaningful manner.

Not meaningful enough for her friend, Mo, who added, 'Together?'

'I always knew there was something special between the two of you,' the third member of their group—Sarra, maybe?—said wistfully.

'Oh, no. Like we told you the other day, we're just friends,' Winter said, a convincingly jolly smile on her face, even though her peaceful spa day was being interrupted. Josh had to admire that kind of dedication to the role.

Skylar leaned forward into Winter's personal space, and rather closer to Josh's bath robe gowned self than he was really comfortable with. 'You can tell us, you know. We wouldn't say anything.'

'We're the souls of discretion,' Sarra agreed, nodding.

Mo looked between them, bemused, which was the most honest reaction Josh could think of, really.

He exchanged a brief glance with Winter and knew already what she was thinking. There was no real way they were going to convince these three otherwise, if they'd decided they were back together. But the last thing they wanted was to give them anything they could use as confirmation—especially since it wasn't even true.

But truth, Josh had learned over the years, didn't tend to matter too much if it got in the way of a good story. And while these three might claim they wouldn't spread the word, Josh knew how that went too. It was too good a titbit not to at least hint at to friends, and then spill, while swearing the friend to secrecy. Then they'd do the same, and soon the buzz would be out there and someone—possibly a colleague of one of the travel journalists staying in this very hotel this very week—would be offering Skylar, Mo and Sarra cash to tell all, and provide photos.

The gossip magazines would have them married again before they'd even finished having enough conversations to find their closure, let alone their new friendship.

When Winter had said they needed to spend their spa break gossiping, he was pretty sure this wasn't what she'd meant.

'Well, I'm done here, anyway.' Josh got to his feet. 'Nice to meet you again, ladies. I'm off to whatever Liam has scheduled next on my agenda. I'll see you later, I'm sure, Winter.'

With a last meaningful look at his ex-wife, he sauntered off as casually as a man in a bathrobe could manage, and hoped she'd got the message.

* * *

Ten minutes later, he was relaxing in the steam room, letting the oils and sinus-opening scents fill his lungs, his head tipped back against the wall, eyes closed as sweat and steam ran down his torso. He smiled when he heard the door open, though, and someone enter very quietly.

'Josh?' Winter called softly.

He opened his eyes. 'Over here.'

She padded over towards him, her bare feet slapping against the wet tiled floor, and took a seat at his side. 'I was assuming you meant for me to meet you here. It was next on my schedule from Liam too.'

'I was hoping it would be,' Josh admitted. 'I thought we might want to continue our... gossiping in private?'

'Definitely,' Winter said with feeling.

Still, it felt almost the wrong place for conversation. They sat together in the darkened steam room, the colour-changing spotlights overhead barely enough to see each other by, and just breathed. Josh could hear Winter's breath pattern mirroring his own, and he realised suddenly this was the most at peace he'd been since she'd left him.

Winter had always meant peace to him.

From the moment he'd spotted her across the set on their first day filming *Fairy Tale of New England,* he'd felt that calmness wash over him just looking at her—and known that she was meant to be in his life.

She still was. And as much as he told himself, and Liam, and anyone else who pressed him for answers, that he wanted to move on— to find that perfect romance, perfect relationship, that the other members of his family had, right now, he wondered.

Would he sacrifice all that if it meant ten more minutes just sitting here, breathing, with Winter?

No. He couldn't. Because losing her had almost broken him last time, and he couldn't put himself, or her, through that again. They just weren't meant to be. If they were, it wouldn't be this hard.

He shook his head instinctively, shaking away the vision and sending droplets of water flying from his hair in Winter's direction.

'Josh!' she squealed.

'Like you're not already soaked through,' he replied, forcing a smile.

Friendship. Closure. That was what he was here for.

Then he could move on and find that real

love of his life he had to believe was out there waiting for him, somewhere.

Because the universe had already made very clear that it wasn't ever going to be Winter.

Spending the day at the spa with Josh was surprisingly fun. After their emotional conversation on the massage tables, and their escape from inquisitive influencers in the manicure room, they'd managed to enjoy the steam room, rainforest and ice walls, sauna, cold plunge pool and the heated stone beds Winter had so been looking forward to.

They ate salads for lunch in their white bathrobes, both of them red-faced and with hair pointing in all directions—a sad result of the massage oil, and constant water since— and the waiter in the spa restaurant even brought them over a carafe of white wine from 'the boss', which they decided it would be rude to waste.

Even reminiscing about their time as a couple didn't hurt as much as she'd thought it might. They'd been together almost from the moment they'd met on set—something the media and fans had made a big deal about. All those 'love at first sight' headlines were perfect for the romantic comedy they'd been filming, so Winter was pretty sure the marketing and publicity team had played them up too.

She and Josh had been too deeply absorbed in each other, and everything growing between them, to pay much attention to the outside world.

Back then, she'd felt everything so acutely—every lingering look from across the set, every smile, every kiss…she'd felt them in her soul.

She hadn't felt *anything* that deeply in five years now. Not even the award nomination she'd worked so damn hard for.

But now she could look back on those days with an outsider's eye, as if she were watching another younger, fresher, more naive girl make those choices, and fall in love. Which, in a way, she was, Winter supposed. Whoever that girl had been, it wasn't her any more.

'I thought we were supposed to be gossiping about the stuff we'd missed over the last few years,' Winter said after a while, when the memories started to sting a little. 'Not reminiscing about stuff we both already know.'

Josh gave her a smile and topped up both of their glasses with the last of the wine.

'Okay, then. Why don't you start by telling me all about how you came to make your latest *award-nominated* movie, Ms Director?'

Winter grinned. This was something she could talk comfortably about. Something that had no connection to Josh, or the past, at all. At least, she thought it didn't.

Until she started talking to him about it.

'After…everything…' a useful shorthand that, to encompass all the things she didn't want to talk about again right now '…I guess I kind of threw myself into my career for a while. Much like you did, I think.' She gave him a knowing look, thinking of the half dozen movies he'd made in record time after their split.

'I guess I can understand that impulse,' he agreed wryly. His fingers twisted the fabric napkin in his hands and she knew that if this were a cheaper establishment, with paper napkins, he'd have shredded it to pieces by now. They were both trying so hard to act as if this was a perfectly normal conversation to be having, a normal situation, but underneath the strain was starting to show. 'For me, being busy stopped me thinking so much. Work was a distraction.'

'So what made you slow down again?' It

was hard not to notice how, after that flurry of movies, he'd hardly been in anything new.

'Burnout,' Josh admitted with a shrug. 'I... I was just done. I went and stayed with my mom and spent time with Graham and Ashley and then the twins when they came along, and just, well, stopped.'

She felt the guilt rising again at that. Guilt that her actions had driven him so far past his limits. But pride in him too, that he'd realised that and taken the time to rest and recover.

'But I was asking about you,' Josh pointed out. 'What made you decide to move behind the camera for a change? I mean, it was obviously a great move—see nomination as noted above and all that. But I don't remember directing ever being something you talked much about. So I have to admit I was kind of surprised when I heard you were directing, not starring in, *Another Time and Place*.'

Winter leant back in her chair, staring out over his shoulder. The restaurant was the only place in the spa that had floor to ceiling windows and she looked out now at the pool beyond—another geothermal lagoon, this one much larger than the private one they shared. It was filled with other guests, all enjoying the warm water, views over the rocky landscape towards the snow-tipped mountains and the slightly sulphurous smell.

She wondered if any of them were watching them back, talking about the two of them having lunch together. Being together. Like the women in the manicure bar had done.

'If you don't want to talk about this, we don't have to.' Josh's brow was crinkled with faint confusion as he gave her the conversational out. Winter could understand why; they'd talked about far more personal, more difficult things without her bailing. Okay, without her bailing *much*.

But this cut to the heart of who she was these days so much more. This wasn't about the Winter she'd left behind. It was key to the Winter she was now. And somehow that made it harder to say out loud.

But she knew she needed to. So she shrugged nonchalantly and turned back to her dessert as if it were no big deal.

'Directing wasn't always a big dream of mine, no,' she admitted. 'But I spent so long having people only talk about me in relation to you—'

'Did they really do that?'

Winter stared at him. 'How could you not

notice? I was always "wife of Josh Abraham" in every article for years.'

'Really? And that was…so bad?' The puzzled look had faded into a stoic, blank mask, and Winter knew that meant her words had stung.

'Not the being married to you part,' she said. 'It wasn't like… I was ashamed of us or you or anything. It was just…'

'You wanted to be your own person,' Josh guessed. 'I can understand that. But, I mean, they talked about me as your husband too, you know.'

'I do know,' Winter said. 'Every article about either of us talked about our fairy tale romance, how we were living the true love dream.' She could hear the bitterness in her voice, and saw it reflected in the dismay that showed on Josh's face.

'I always thought that was…well. I liked it.' Josh gave a strange sort of half shrug. 'I liked that our love story was epic. That people saw it as a fairy tale.'

Of course he had. Because, for him, that was exactly what he'd always wanted—a love story to rival his parents' and his brother's.

But for her…

'It wasn't that I didn't love our story, and

that it resonated with people,' she said carefully. 'I just didn't want it to be the only thing people thought of when they saw me.'

'So you took yourself off camera,' Josh said.

'I guess I figured that if no one was ever going to talk about my acting, I'd try something else.' Something where audiences weren't staring at her all the time, thinking about how she'd walked out on her true love. How she'd betrayed him.

How she'd lost their child.

Because of course that had been all over the papers too. Suddenly, she'd become a figure of pity, not one of envy, and it turned out she didn't like that any better either.

'You never said anything,' he said. 'Back then. You never told me you felt that way.'

'I didn't know how,' Winter admitted. 'You...you loved the fairy tale. It was everything you ever wanted. And saying that it wasn't what *I* wanted... It would have sounded like I didn't want *you,* and that was never the problem.'

She'd said too much, she realised, snapping her jaw closed. But she *had* always wanted him. That wasn't something that changed. It was just everything else that had.

Josh was studying her with a sudden heat in his eyes at her words, when in a flash his attention and gaze jerked away, to something over her shoulder. She turned too, and saw the women from earlier entering the restaurant.

'Time to move on?' Josh said, and she nodded, gathering up her things, even as she knew that this conversation wasn't fully over.

Josh leaned against the open doorway of Liam's office a few hours later, his hair still wet and his shirt sticking to his back from where he'd dressed too hurriedly after his time in the spa. But he'd wanted to speak to his friend, and urgently.

'How was the spa?' Liam asked, motioning him into the office.

Josh closed the door behind him and took his usual seat in the armchair by the window. 'Luxurious.'

'Relaxing?'

'In parts.'

'And the company?' The innocence in Liam's voice was definitely fake.

Josh gave him a look. 'We talked some,' he said. 'But not enough. Too many people watching.'

'I did give you a private lagoon for your

conversations,' Liam pointed out. 'I mean, really, I got you both here in the first place. What more do you want from me?'

Just the question Josh had been pondering as he'd sat in the steam room and laughed at Winter jumping into the cold plunge pool afterwards.

The conversation they'd had at lunchtime wasn't the end of it, Josh was sure about that. Learning that she'd found the media interpretation of their story as a fairy tale, as true love, annoying had hurt. But at the same time he was beginning to understand her point of view at least. He could get how frustrating it must have been for her to only ever be seen in her relationship to him.

And that wouldn't change as long as they were both here, in full sight of all the journalists, bloggers and influencers Liam had invited to the Ice House for the week.

So, what did he want from Liam?

'I want your help getting Winter away from here for the night, somewhere we can hang out and talk in private. Somewhere fun.'

Liam's eyebrows leapt up at that. 'Because you're trying to *woo* her back to you again?'

'I knew that last period drama you did was

a mistake,' Josh grumbled. 'I'm not *wooing* anybody.'

'Which is, I believe, part of the problem we're trying to fix here. Isn't it?' The eyebrows were still raised.

'Yes. Obviously.' Josh hoped he didn't sound as if he'd forgotten the objective for the week, even though he had.

He was here to find closure with Winter and move on so he could find true love again with someone else and stop obsessing over why his fairy tale romance hadn't ended in a happy ever after. And talking to Winter some more about how she'd felt when they were married was part of that.

That was all.

Nothing to do with wanting to see her let down her guard again and laugh with him. To see her smile across a table in candlelight like there was nowhere else in the world she wanted to be.

Nothing to do with any of that at all. Because that way lay heartbreak and burnout. Again.

'So you just want to take her out somewhere tonight on a friend date?'

'Yes. Exactly that. Except not a date at all. Just…we need to talk some more, away from watching eyes. And we've spent the whole day at the spa, so I think an evening in the lagoon is off the cards.'

Liam didn't ask why they couldn't just use one of their private suites, for which he was grateful. He didn't have much of an answer beyond needing to be on neutral territory.

And maybe somewhere neither of them could just run easily if the conversation grew hard.

Liam surveyed him across the desk, his gaze thoughtful. Josh wasn't sure exactly what his friend was looking for, but it seemed he found it because, after a long moment, he nodded.

'Okay, then. The pair of you meet me at the side entrance in an hour. I'll get you out of here.'

'You're not going to tell me where we're going?' Josh asked. Liam's idea of a perfect friends' night out was not necessarily the same as his. He'd have to warn Winter that wherever they ended up was all Liam's doing…

'It's a surprise.' Liam flashed him a grin and picked up his phone. 'Just trust me, okay. Don't worry. I'll tell Jenny the plan so she can help Winter choose an appropriate outfit.'

'What about *my* outfit?' Josh asked.

Liam rolled his eyes. 'My friend, you have been in Hollywood too long. Now, go figure out how you're going to woo your ex-wife back.'

'That's not what I'm doing.'

A knowing, slightly smug smile spread across Liam's face. 'Of course it isn't. Now, go!'

Josh was so busy denying Liam's accusations in his head he was almost back at his suite before he thought to wonder when Liam had got Jenny's phone number.

CHAPTER EIGHT

'WHY WILL NOBODY tell me where I'm going?'
Winter asked the moment she opened the
door of her suite to Josh that evening.

'Trust me, if I knew I'd tell you,' he replied
with a shrug. 'I remember how much you
hate surprises. But I'm afraid our gracious
host hasn't seen fit to share his plans for our
evening with me.'

Winter shot a glare back into the room at
Jenny, who was trying to look innocent on
the sofa. '*Jenny* knows.'

'Apparently our Liam is keener on sharing things with Jenny than either of us,' Josh
said drily. Then he dropped his voice. 'You
know we don't have to go, if you don't want
to. I just thought it might be a good way to
get away from here and finish our conversation from earlier.'

She couldn't deny that she liked the idea of
getting away from all the people who seemed

to be watching her every movement here at the hotel. Plus, she *had* got all dressed up now.'

'Oh, come on then.' She grabbed her coat and bag. 'Don't wait up!' Winter was pretty sure Jenny would hear the sarcasm in that one. If not, the way she slammed the door behind her probably did it.

Liam wasn't waiting for them at the side entrance, but a long black car with tinted windows was. The black-capped driver opened the rear doors for them, and they both slipped inside.

'I don't suppose you want to give us a clue where we're going tonight?' Winter asked him before he shut her door.

He gave her a not entirely reassuring amused smile in return.

'Liam really didn't tell you where he's sending us?' Winter asked as the car pulled away from the hotel.

'Not a clue,' Josh replied, looking a little concerned. 'But he said it would be somewhere we could talk in private, without worrying about being watched.'

'That's something, I suppose.' Winter settled back in her seat and watched the blackness of the Icelandic night passing by.

They were on the road back into Reykjavik, she realised. Maybe Liam had booked them a table at a private restaurant or something. That would be okay.

She and Josh tried to make small talk, but the apprehension that hung over both of them made it difficult and they soon lapsed into silence, long before they entered the city.

Then, eventually, the car came to a stop in front of a building. Except it didn't look like a restaurant. And the windows were mostly in darkness.

'Are you sure this is the right place?' Josh asked.

The driver was openly grinning now. 'Oh, for sure. Mr Delaney arranged for them to open this evening for you especially.'

Why did Winter have such a bad feeling about this?

She climbed out of the car, took Josh's arm, then looked up at the sign on the building in front of them.

The Icelandic Phallological Museum.

Of course.

Beside her, Josh was blinking very hard. 'Has Liam...has he sent us on a date to a museum full of...'

'Penises,' said a well-dressed woman who'd suddenly appeared in the doorway in front of them. 'That's right! We're probably the only museum in the world to include a specimen penis from every land and sea mammal found in our country. Please come in!'

The driver was already pulling away from the kerb, leaving them no escape route. Winter exchanged a slightly panicked look with Josh, who shrugged, making it clear it was her call.

'Well, okay then.' Winter pulled her faux-fur coat tighter around her. 'Let's take a look.'

Once they'd got over their initial embarrassment at Liam's choice of an appropriate date location—even if it wasn't really a date—Winter had to admit, the Icelandic Phallological Museum was genuinely interesting. Even if she and Josh couldn't help but snigger at a few of the exhibits.

'Did you see the size of the sperm whale?' Josh whispered to her, and Winter giggled as she nodded.

The museum was officially closed for the day, so they had the whole place to themselves, the museum worker who'd greeted them discreetly leaving them to browse the huge collection alone. For once, they didn't have to worry about anybody seeing them together or jumping to conclusions, but they were having too much fun to waste that opportunity on deep and meaningful conversations.

It felt…freeing. Fun.

By the time they'd taken in all the exhibits, Winter's stomach was starting to rumble. They wandered over to the abandoned café to find one table set out with a white tablecloth and candles she suspected didn't get much use in the museum day to day.

While Josh considered a pint of Moby Dick ale or a 'cockaccino' she surveyed the variety of penis-themed treats available in the nearby gift shop. Clearly this place had found a niche and really gone for it.

She kind of loved it.

Even if she was going to kill Liam for sending them there. The man was the opposite of subtle.

Except…it wasn't as if there was anything sexual about the museum at all, despite its premise. And actually, surveying the exhibits with Josh, giggling about animal genitalia… it had been *fun*. It had broken all the tension between them and given them a break from the difficult conversations they'd been having all week.

Maybe Liam had known what he was doing after all.

Not that she'd ever tell him that.

The museum café served them penis calzone followed by phallic-shaped waffles topped with berries and cream. While it wasn't exactly the gourmet dinner out Josh had been expecting when he'd asked Liam to arrange their date, he had to admit it was a lot more entertaining. And it had lightened the mood between them—something Josh hadn't been certain was possible after the conversations of the last few days, despite their best efforts in the spa.

They kept the small talk light and inconsequential over dinner, still giggling about their favourite exhibits, or the mug Winter had found in the gift shop.

It wasn't until they were sipping their coffees—with penis-shaped patterns in the foam, obviously—that he returned at all to their earlier unfinished conversation. And even that felt lighter. More...flirtatious, even—not that he'd admit that to Liam, or mention it to Winter, for fear of breaking the spell.

'So, you like directing?' he asked.

Winter nodded, placing her cup back in its saucer. 'I do. More than I thought I would. I mean... I think I was just challenging myself to try something new originally. And maybe...maybe hiding a little by being behind the camera instead of in front of it. But mostly it was, you know, throwing myself into my career because I'd been such a failure at the personal side of things, that old cliché.'

'Right.' It might be a cliché, but Josh's chest still tightened at the casual way she said it. *Such a failure.* As if it was an established, un-arguable fact about her—the same way her black hair or green eyes were.

Except it wasn't true. *He* was the failure. Not her.

He was the one who hadn't been there when she'd needed him. Who she hadn't been able to talk to about how she was feeling. He'd failed as a husband, and it had cost him everything.

But Winter carried on, oblivious to his startled musings.

'But I really enjoyed it. I liked being able to tell a whole story, not just my part in it. I liked having that sort of control too—to put across things that mattered to me. Have you seen it? *Another Time and Place*, I mean.'

Josh started. 'Of course I've seen it. You think I wouldn't go see your first movie as a director?'

Was the pinkness in her cheeks just due to the coffee? He hoped not.

'What did you think?' Her voice was small, uncertain, and Josh couldn't help but smile at it.

'The award nomination wasn't enough for your ego?'

She shook her head. 'It's not… Awards aren't everything, you and I both know that. I want to know what *you* think.'

A warmth filled him at the idea that his opinion still mattered to her. That she thought about what *he* thought at all.

'I loved it,' he said honestly. 'I thought it was smart, and funny, and touching and *real*. And I could feel *you* in every frame of it.'

Her blush had gone from a faint tint to bright red now, and Josh realised he loved that too.

'Thank you,' she said softly. Her eyes looked a little wet.

'It must have been a hell of a lot of work, though,' he said, giving her a moment to rec-ollect herself. 'I mean, it's such an…intense movie. So closely focused on your characters, and the setting. I know how demanding that kind of movie is to act in. I can't imagine *di-recting* one.'

Winter nodded. 'Yeah. I mean, I know we didn't have all the green screen effects or the action sequences or what have you. But mak-ing it powerful enough to stand without any of that stuff that audiences have come to ex-pect…that was its own challenge. I was lucky with my cast, though. Melody especially—she really got what I was trying to say with the film, and she knocked it out of the park.'

'She did.' What she'd said about Melody, though...that had him thinking. 'The story you chose to tell... I heard the reporter at the press conference asking you about second chance love. Finding love again after loss, or divorce, or whatever. Was that... I mean... were you...' He trailed off, the words eluding him.

Winter seemed to know what he meant, though. She always had, until the end, when neither of them had enough words left to express all the terrible things they were feeling.

He'd thought that he'd understood her the same way. Apparently he'd been wrong.

'You mean was that a personal story to tell?' She raised her eyebrows at him with a smile. 'Am I searching for love again?'

'Yeah, I guess.' The idea of it made his heart hurt. But wasn't he doing exactly the same? Trying to find closure with Winter so he could move on for a second chance at love? He could hardly blame her for wanting exactly the same thing he did.

But Winter shook her head. 'No. I'm not... dating, or whatever. I'm focusing on my career and that's enough for me right now.'

'But one day?' Oh, God, why was he pushing it? Maybe so he could ignore the huge surge of relief that ran through him at her words.

'Perhaps,' she said with a light shrug, but she sounded unconvinced.

And that surge of relief turned into a tsunami, even as the guilt that came with it grew.

He should want her to move on. To find happiness again.

It was just...the thought of her falling for another guy the way she'd fallen for him. Of her experiencing all that heady emotion, the days where all they could see was each other, when other people and whole film sets disappeared and the world shrank to just the two of them. Those can't-keep-our-hands-off-each-other days, those share-all-our-secrets-in-whispers nights, and everything in between them.

He wanted that again. And he wanted her to have that again.

He just couldn't quite imagine either of them having it with anyone else.

And that...that was a problem.

Josh's gaze had turned glassy, as if he was occupying a world she wasn't part of. Lost inside his head, she supposed, now they were back on more dicey topics. Like her love life—or total lack of.

Was he disappointed she hadn't moved on? Had he hoped that she'd say she was out there on the dating scene and free him from any residual guilt about doing the same? That would be like Josh—a gentleman to the end, and not willing to move on from their fairy tale until she did.

Or...

No. She couldn't let herself think about that. The possibility that maybe he *didn't* want her to move on because he hadn't either.

She should change the subject. Talk about his next movie, or sperm whale penises, or *anything* that wasn't their love lives.

'What about you?' The words were out before she could stop them. 'Are you dating right now? I haven't seen many photos of you with anyone—not serious someone's anyway. But then, I haven't really been looking.'

'No, there's...no one.' He looked down at the remains of the foam in his coffee as he shook his head. 'First I was just working all the time, and then I was at Mom's, and since then...'

He looked up suddenly, his gaze catching hers like a hook, and the heat in it made her swallow, hard.

'There's no one,' he finished. But she heard all the words he didn't say—because she was thinking them too.

There's no one like you. There could never be anyone like you.

Oh, but she was screwed.

She couldn't do this. Couldn't risk falling again like this. She should have run the moment she'd realised her heart still skipped when she saw him.

She should never have come to Iceland at all.

'We should get going.' She pushed her chair out from the table and stumbled quickly to her feet. 'God only knows what Liam has planned for us tomorrow, but I doubt it will be as restful as today's spa activities.'

'Yeah, you're right.' Josh stood too, more gracefully than she'd managed. 'I just want to grab something from the gift shop first.'

When he'd paid for his purchases—a penis mug for her and a museum logo T-shirt for himself—plus a whole bag of gummy penises for Liam—they made their way back out front, thanking the museum employees who'd stayed late to give them their unusual evening together.

It was very late, she realised as the driver opened the car door for her. They must have talked for hours and, now they'd stopped, her tiredness was catching up with her. She dozed in the car back to the hotel, leaning on Josh's arm gratefully as he helped her out of the car at the other end.

They sneaked in through the side door and made their way through the dimly lit hallways of the hotel, towards their adjoining suites.

But when she reached her room she realised that, despite all her good intentions, she wasn't quite ready to say goodnight yet. Maybe she shouldn't have come to Iceland at all. But now she was here...she couldn't just ignore this moment.

It might be the last one she ever got with him.

'Thank you for tonight,' she said softly, leaning against the wood of her door.

'I think you have Liam to thank for the romantic location,' he joked. 'But thank *you* for your company. It was nice to have some time alone, just us.'

'Just us and over two hundred penises,' she pointed out, making him laugh.

'Yes. Can't forget the penises. Speaking of which...' He handed her the mug he'd bought at the gift shop. 'Can't forget this either.'

She pulled it from the bag and studied it

with amusement. 'Ah, yes. Thank you for my…thoughtful gift.'

They shared another smile, and in it Winter could feel so many things that neither of them were saying. Or *could* say.

They were past all that. She'd walked out and left it five years ago and she couldn't honestly believe that there was a path back, even if she wanted to walk it.

This felt like goodbye. A real one this time.

But then he leaned in to place a kiss on her cheek, whispering, 'Goodnight, Winter,' against her skin.

'Goodnight,' she murmured back. And then, before she could stop herself, she turned her face and caught his lips with her own.

For a long moment she lost herself in the kiss—in the warmth of his mouth on hers, the way his free hand came to clutch at her hip as he met her kiss with his own, deepening it, sweeping his tongue across her lower lip in the way she'd always loved. She let the heat build between them, let him press her against the closed door, rejoiced in the length of him full against her, felt him harden against her stomach—

He pulled away.

'Winter.' Josh rested his arm above her head on the door, looking down at her with

darkened eyes. He looked…wrecked. 'I…
We…'

'Right. Of course.' It *had* been goodbye.
And she'd ruined it.

'I'm just saying—'

'No, you're right!' She spun out from under
his arm, fishing in her clutch bag for her room
key card, relieved when it slid into the lock
and turned green first time. 'I need to sleep.
I'll see you tomorrow.'

She opened the door only enough to slip
through, then shut it fast and tight behind her,
hoping it wasn't loud enough to wake Jenny.

Then she leaned against it and listened for
Josh's footsteps walking away.

CHAPTER NINE

JOSH DIDN'T SLEEP MUCH.

How could he, after that kiss? After he'd held Winter in his arms again, even with that damn penis mug still dangling from her fingers.

He'd wanted to say so much, once he'd broken the kiss. But the words just wouldn't come. Maybe there *weren't* words for all the things he was feeling. But he had to find some that would do if he wanted Winter to understand.

The pain in her eyes when he'd pulled away...he'd known instantly that he'd done the wrong thing, again. That she'd misunderstood. That she'd thought he didn't want this when, in reality, it was the only thing he ever had wanted.

The last five years he'd thought he'd been moving on, but the whole time he'd been hanging on to the possibility of *this* and he hadn't even realised.

But giving in to it...

Josh wasn't sure he could handle the pain it might bring when he had to say goodbye again. Because they already knew they didn't work together.

As the clock ticked over towards morning, he gave up on even dozing a little longer and dragged himself from the comfort of bed. His shower woke him up a little at least, and he dressed quickly and headed for breakfast in search of coffee.

There was no sign of Winter or Jenny in the restaurant, which didn't really surprise him—he imagined they'd have room service again, especially after last night. But he'd only been sitting alone at his window table, nursing a black Americano with no foam to have penises drawn in, for a short time when Liam slid into the chair opposite him.

'How was your date last night?' he asked, a smile dancing around his lips.

Josh raised his eyebrows. 'You mean our guided tour of the penis museum?'

That drew a full-blown laugh from his friend. 'I'm sorry, I couldn't resist. And I thought it would be a good ice-breaker, at least.'

'It was,' Josh admitted. 'It definitely lightened the mood, anyway.'

'It's hard to be too serious when you're surrounded by two hundred plus animal penises,' Liam replied sagely. 'So, it went well?'

'Mostly.' He didn't want to get into how things had ended right now. 'Oh, and I bought you these.' Josh handed over the bag of gummy penises and earned himself another laugh.

'Just what I always wanted,' Liam said.

'So, what's on the agenda for today?' Josh half hoped that Liam would say that there was nothing planned, and they could have a free day. Maybe then he could drag Winter out to the private lagoon and they could talk some more about last night's kiss.

On the other hand, being around her in a two-piece swimsuit right now, trying to talk, might be a little more than his fragile sense of self-restraint could take.

'The Golden Circle,' Liam said with a grin. 'Geysers and waterfalls and iconic landmarks—oh, my!'

'Sounds great,' Josh said unconvincingly. At least it meant Winter would be wrapped up under plenty of layers of clothing for warmth. Maybe that would make it easier for him to concentrate while they talked.

'It will be,' Liam promised. 'Trust me, you

haven't seen anything until you visit Gullfoss in full flow.'

Liam had arranged a coach to take them all around the Golden Circle, although a far fancier one than Josh suspected most people took this tour on. He'd taken his seat early, and used the free Wi-Fi to read up a bit on the tour on his phone. Not much of the information would be retained though, he suspected, since his attention kept drifting out of the window, looking for Winter.

But there was no sign.

As the coach filled up, his concern grew. Had she decided not to come at all? Was she that desperate to avoid him?

He was just about to disembark and go looking for her, when he spotted the multi-coloured pompom on the top of Winter's bobble hat, and Jenny's blonde head bobbing behind her.

There was an empty pair of seats in front of him, but Winter and Jenny bypassed them without looking at him, heading instead for seats towards the back. Josh watched them go, then glared at Liam when he took the empty seat beside him.

'Looks like last night might not have gone quite as well as you thought, mate,' Liam said.

Ignoring him, Josh hunkered down in his seat and began plotting his next moves.

'Are you absolutely certain nothing happened last night that you need to tell me about?' Jenny's eyebrows were raised but her voice was low, obviously conscious of all the other guests sitting around them.

'I told you,' Winter replied testily. 'We went to the penis museum. It was ridiculous. We came home. That was all.'

Jenny's sceptical gaze felt uncomfortable on her face, so Winter turned away to look out of the window at the passing landscape instead.

Snow had fallen again in the night and the rocky ground outside and its sparse grass covering was turned white. The roads were still clear, though—a testament to a good infrastructure that was used to the colder weather, she supposed.

She wondered what their lagoon would be like in the snow, if they met out there tonight. Whether the flakes would melt on impact with the warmer water. Whether she and Josh would cuddle closer to stay warm and watch it fall. Whether he'd put his arm around her. Whether he'd kiss her again...

No. She wasn't thinking about that. She

was thinking about Iceland's Golden Circle and listening to Liam talk into the microphone at the front of the bus about the exciting sites they'd be visiting today.

She was not imagining kissing her ex-husband again.

Or more than just kissing…

Dammit! *Not thinking about this.*

She couldn't afford to. Giving in to her desires with Josh could only lead to her regressing into the person she'd been—losing all the change and growth she'd fought so hard for. Wouldn't it?

With a shake of her head, Winter forced herself to focus in again on Liam's tour guide patter until they reached their first destination—Þingvellir National Park. Although, as she couldn't remember a word of what she was supposed to look out for there when they arrived, she had to admit she might have drifted off a bit.

The others headed straight into the visitor centre, presumably to supplement Liam's talk with the official guide—and avoid freezing in the bitter air—but Winter stayed outside, staring out over the strange geology of the place.

Below her viewing point, the land seemed cracked in two deep fissures running through the rock and earth. Snowflakes fell either side of them, and deep down into the gaps. Across the other side of the canyon, behind a large lake, she could see a small white church, and a house the same colour, both almost invisible against the white-grey of the snow-laden sky.

'This is the point where two continents meet.' Josh's voice made her jump, and she turned quickly to find him a few paces away, watching her. 'A fault line between the Eurasian and North American plates.'

'A bit like you and me then,' Winter said, turning back to the incredible view. 'Your American versus my British heritage.' Their upbringing and nationality had never really seemed a rift between them before, but suddenly Winter found she needed to focus on all the things that separated them, rather than the things they had in common.

It was safer that way.

If she thought too much about the things that brought them together...well. She'd seen where that had ended last night. And she knew how *that* sort of thing had ended last time.

Better not to risk it again.

'There's constant earthquakes here,' Josh went on, his voice growing ever closer. 'But they're too minor to feel them.'

She didn't need to turn around to know he

was right behind her now. In fact, if she did turn, she'd probably find herself in his arms.

Winter forced herself to stay put.

'And it was the site of Iceland's first general assembly—the start of a representative parliament, all the way back in the tenth century.' Was he just going to keep spouting facts about this place until she spoke to him? Probably.

'You were listening to Liam's talk on the coach,' she said. 'You know I was there for that too?'

'But were you listening?'

She shrugged, although the movement was probably completely hidden by the bulk of her warmest waterproof padded coat. 'It was hard to hear at the back of the bus.'

Or she'd just been too preoccupied to concentrate.

Josh sighed and moved beside her. Peeking sideways, she saw him fold his arms over his chest as he surveyed the view of the rift below. 'Well, it's no penis museum...'

'But it is pretty impressive,' Winter finished, flashing him a quick smile.

He reached out to grab her gloved hand. 'Winter. About last night—'

She pulled away before he could continue. 'We don't need to talk about that. In fact I'd rather forget it. And, anyway, it's cold out here. I want to see the visitor centre before Liam orders us all back on the bus.'

Without looking back, she strode away towards the visitor centre and its fascinating exhibitions on the geology and history of Iceland.

Because right now Josh and her relationship with him felt far too much like the landscape of this place. Fractured, unstable and drifting apart—but still so damn compelling she found it hard to look away.

Winter was definitely avoiding him. Or avoiding talking about the kiss. Or both.

And trying to talk to her without the whole bus watching—or eavesdropping—was growing impossible anyway.

Their next stop on the Golden Circle tour was Geysir, where they watched spouts of hot air burst from the ground into the snowy sky from the Strokkur Geysir. Then, once they were all shivering again and the joy of the water spurts had worn off, it was back on the coach towards Gullfoss.

The landscape of Iceland was unlike anything he'd ever seen before, outside of the movies and TV shows that had filmed there. Everything felt unfamiliar, unstable—and it wasn't helping him feel any more settled or centred in himself, or in the new friendship he was trying to build with Winter.

Friendship? Who was he kidding? Whatever Liam had hoped to achieve by bringing them both here, there could never be just friendship between Josh and Winter. They both felt too much—and had been hurt too badly—for that.

But what did that leave them?

Having found her again, Josh wasn't sure he could just let her go. Not when he'd felt more being with her in three days in Iceland than he had in the five years without her.

Not when her kiss could still light up his whole world the way it had last night.

They weren't meant for marriage. They couldn't do the whole fairy tale thing, they'd proven that.

Everything he'd thought he wanted his whole life—everything he'd thought he'd found with Winter before she'd left him... could he forget about that? Could he accept something else, something less, in its place?

He wasn't sure. But it looked as if he was going to have to decide. And fast. They only had limited time left in Iceland, then Winter would be walking away from him again. If he didn't want that to happen…well. He had to get her to talk to him, for a start.

The big question was, which would be worse? The lifelong regret if he didn't at least try to have *something* with her one last time, or the pain that would come when he inevitably had to watch her walk away again?

Josh wasn't sure there was a good answer to that one.

The final stop on the Golden Circle tour was the waterfall of Gullfoss. The coach pulled into the car park near the wooden-clad visitor centre, but this time nobody rushed inside. Everyone wanted to see the famous waterfall first.

Josh followed behind them, watching as Winter and Jenny picked their careful way along the wooden slatted path towards the viewing point, wary of any icy patches. The snow had settled on the ground around the waterfall and on any of the rocks that pushed through from the river bed, but the water flowed around it without disturbing it. On the far side of the falls, where even the weak winter sun didn't reach, ice had formed, a strange solid contrast to the rushing roar of the waterfalls. Steam rose up from the ravine where the racing, cascading falls hit the icy river water below.

As he moved to the wooden rail of the platform, jutting out over the very edge of the ravine itself, the roar became louder, so loud he couldn't make out the conversations of anyone around him.

And that gave him an idea.

Already, members of their group were starting to turn to head back to the warmth of the visitor centre. Josh watched them go until only a handful were left, then made his way towards where Winter stood alone at the rail.

Nobody watching would know or care who they were, not through the mist rising off the waterfall, and the bulky clothes and hats they both wore. And nobody would be able to hear a word he said.

It was the most privacy they were likely to get until they were back at their rooms—and there he had no guarantee she'd talk to him at all.

'We need to talk.' He had to get close to Winter, his mouth almost at her ear, to be sure she'd hear him over the roar of the water, but apparently she'd been so distracted by the view she hadn't realised he was there, because she jumped at his voice.

'I can't hear you,' she lied. 'It'll have to wait.'

'Nobody is watching. Nobody can hear us.

Trust me, this is the best chance we're going to get.'

He could see the indecision in her eyes, in the way her gaze darted over her shoulder to look who else was around.

'What if I'm just not ready for this conversation?'

He had to read her lips to catch her words, but they prompted an ironic smile, anyway.

'Winter. It's been five years. If not now, when?'

She didn't answer, so he took her silence as permission to plough on with what he had to say.

'I've been thinking about this all day. Since the moment I left you outside your room last night. From the second your lips left mine. And all I can think is… I can't bear the thought of a world where I never get to kiss you again.'

Her sharp intake of breath told him that, whatever she'd expected, it wasn't that.

'I know we failed at marriage.' *He* failed. 'I know we can't have the fairy tale. But maybe that isn't what I need any more,' he pressed on.

'Yes. It is.' More lip-reading, her words torn away by the wind and the water. 'You know it is. And I can't give that to you.'

She was right. He knew she was right. It just didn't seem to matter any more.

When he'd realised she'd gone, when he'd found that letter five years ago, the pain had been unbearable. He'd blocked a lot of it out, over the months and years that followed. But one thing had stuck with him.

I didn't know it was the last time.

The last time they'd kissed. The last time they'd made love. The last time she'd smiled at him. The last time she'd told him she loved him.

Some of them he couldn't even remember. And even those he did…he hadn't known.

Hadn't known that he'd never experience that again.

That it was the last time.

And if he *had* known…maybe he couldn't have changed anything. But he'd have paid better attention. Savoured the moment more. Committed every second to memory, so he'd always have a piece of it with him.

Winter leaving without warning had taken that from him. But now…

Now he wondered if he could get something of that back.

They had only a few days left in Iceland. Days in which he could relive those last times, if she let him. And after that…

Well. One step at a time. First he had to convince her.

'You can give me something else, though,' he said desperately. 'You can give me something more. Maybe that closure we were looking for wasn't a goodbye. That's not enough for me. I need you again.'

CHAPTER TEN

I NEED YOU AGAIN.

Josh's words were whipped away by the wind, but somehow they still echoed in her brain as she tried to make sense of them.

The confusion in his eyes told her that he didn't understand this pull between them any more than she did.

She'd walked away. She'd spent five years rebuilding her life without him. And now...

Now all she wanted was to kiss him again.

'Until we're able to say goodbye?' Winter's eyes must be wide, because she could feel the chill of the air against them as she stared at him. 'You mean...find a way to finish things properly?'

'One last time,' Josh whispered, so close to her ear that she could feel his breath against its shell, could hear him even over the roaring water.

It wouldn't be enough—she knew that instinctively. But if that was what he needed to move on…

'Real closure,' she murmured to herself.

This was what they'd been missing all along. She could see that now. What she'd robbed them of by running the way she had.

She hadn't been able to face him, or her feelings, back then. But this week…they'd done that, together. They'd faced everything together. Said all the things they'd held back.

All that was left was to say goodbye.

'You're right,' she said, louder. 'Everything between us…it ended so abruptly. And those last months with the pregnancy and the sickness and the miscarriage and afterwards… Maybe what we need is to finish things properly.'

One last time for good luck…

He used to say that, before kissing her goodbye when he left for a shoot.

'I say we try it.' He smiled at her, the icy wind turning his cheeks red, and she returned it.

They could do this. *She* could do this. Otherwise, what had the last five years even been for?

'Then meet me in the lagoon tonight,' she said.

Winter had thought she'd have to wait until Jenny went to bed, or come up with some excuse why she wanted to go out to the lagoon alone that evening. But, to her surprise, her assistant disappeared after dinner without any explanation for her absence, and Winter was able to sneak outside in her bikini and towelling robe, two mugs of her famous hot chocolate in hand, unobserved.

Except for Josh. He was already waiting in the private lagoon, his bare torso mostly hidden by the dark and the water, but his arms outstretched over the rocks holding himself in place. Winter let her gaze run across the muscles of his arms and shoulders—God, she'd always loved those shoulders—before meeting his gaze and smiling at the heat already on display there.

She had no idea what she was doing, she freely admitted that. But she was damned if she could bring herself to stop.

'I brought hot chocolate,' she said, waving the mugs slightly before placing them on the side.

'Hot chocolate always helps,' Josh replied. 'Now, get in here before you freeze.'

She slipped the robe from her shoulders, wincing at the biting cold before she stepped into the water. The heat of the geothermal pool soon warmed her skin, but she found herself floating towards Josh all the same, the desire to share body heat impossible to ignore.

'How do you want to do this?' She looked up at him, his blue eyes so dark against the night sky—or maybe it was the lust covering them. And suddenly the double meaning of her words hit and her mind was filled with every sexual position they'd ever tried, every place they'd ever made love, every moment they'd ever been touching...

'Winter, I—' He broke off, clearly as unable to find the words as she was.

Maybe they didn't need words any more. Perhaps they'd said them all already.

She lurched towards his lips, trusting him to catch her, which he did, his strong arms wrapping tight around her waist in an instant. And then she was kissing him again, and she knew this couldn't be a bad idea because it felt... So. Damn. Right.

This time, Josh didn't break away—she did, and only because she needed to gulp more air into her lungs.

'Are you sure?' he whispered against the skin of her neck, as he kissed his way down towards her collarbone. 'This isn't what either of us came to Iceland for.'

'But it's what we need,' she finished for him. His head jerked up and his gaze met hers, and she knew they were on the same page for the first time in years.

'It really, really is.'

She could feel how much he needed it, even in the water. Somehow, she'd ended up straddling his lap as they kissed, her knees knocking up against the rock wall of the lagoon. His hardness pressed up against the core of her, and she knew that wasn't going to be enough for her, not for long.

'Should we take this inside to your room?' The words came out breathy, and he smiled a slow, special smile—one she'd only ever seen him smile at her, usually in intimate moments like this. Even when she'd studied his sex scenes on film, that particular smile had never been on display.

It was hers.

And God, how she'd missed it.

'Not yet,' he murmured back, his mouth at her throat again. 'I've been having a lot of thoughts about this lagoon this week, you know. It seems a shame not to make some of them reality, while we're here.'

It was too cold for them to stay out there long, Winter knew. Unless he'd suddenly gained the ability to breathe underwater, his kisses were never going to make it below the straps of her bikini, and she definitely wanted his mouth on more of her than that. But he was right that this was a once in a lifetime opportunity...

She nodded, and instantly his hands went to the thin pieces of material holding her bikini top in place.

'I hope this place is as private as Liam promised,' she joked as he stripped the fabric away from her breasts.

'You're under the water anyway,' Josh reassured her. 'Besides, in a landscape like this, a lagoon like this, what could be more natural?'

His hands came up to cup her breasts as she adjusted her position, sitting on his knees to give him better access. The milky water hid everything lower than her waist from view, but she could see his fingers brushing against her nipples with perfect clarity in the moonlight.

'Turn around,' he whispered against her ear.

Swallowing, Winter obeyed.

He felt so hard against her, even through his swim shorts and her bikini bottoms, that she couldn't help but imagine how he'd feel inside her again after so long.

Josh moved his hands back to her bare breasts, thrumming his fingers against her nipples in the way she'd always loved. His mouth was back at her throat, kissing the sensitive skin between her neck and her shoulder, and Winter knew the heat building inside her now had nothing to do with any geothermal power.

It was all him.

It was *them.* The way it always had been.

How did I ever walk away from this?

No, she wasn't thinking about that now. This couldn't last for ever, so she intended to enjoy every second of it.

His right hand drifted lower, between her legs, and she let her head fall back against his shoulder as his touch worked to both relieve and build the heat and the want growing there. And soon there was nothing in the world except that tightness building inside her, her whole body reaching for something that felt just out of reach, straining and desperate, the muscles in her legs tense as she braced herself, hoping and wanting and—

She broke against his fingers, the swell of her orgasm overcoming her as she fell boneless against him.

Josh chuckled warmly against her ear. 'Okay. *Now* we can move this inside. Your bed or mine?'

Josh awoke in his own bed the next morning, knowing that the whole world had changed overnight. And even if that knowledge hadn't been innate, the dark head pillowed against his shoulder and the pale, smooth arm wrapped around his torso would have filled him in fast enough.

He'd slept with Winter. He'd taken his ex-wife back into his bed, five years after she'd broken his heart for good, and he had absolutely no regrets. Except, perhaps, that she was still asleep and he couldn't do it all over again.

Regrets were for later. He couldn't let himself go down that path now.

A knock at the door made him tense as Winter stirred in his arms, then settled down again. He waited, hoping whoever it was would go away, but then they knocked again. With a frustrated sigh, Josh gently disentangled himself from Winter, pulled on a pair of boxers and stalked across to the door.

'What?' he asked in a harsh whisper as he opened the door just a crack—and found Liam's smiling face on the other side.

'You realise you're missing a guided tour of Reykjavik right now? And you missed breakfast,' Liam said, too innocently. 'I thought I'd better check everything was okay.'

'Everything is fine.' The words came out through gritted teeth, as Josh tried not to wake

Winter. It might only be Liam at the door this time, but she'd made her wish to keep whatever this was between them well under the radar.

'Are you sure?' Liam pressed, grinning. 'Only it turns out that *Winter* missed breakfast, and the tour too. And Jenny says she doesn't think she came back to their suite either. All. Night.'

Josh stepped into the corridor and pulled the handle of the door up so it wouldn't lock behind him. Luckily their rooms were on a secluded corridor away from the others, so the chances of being spotted in his boxers were slim, especially if the others were all off on today's tour.

'We're…trying something new,' Josh told his friend.

Liam raised an eyebrow. 'Sex? Honestly, Josh, it's really not that new. Unless you're doing something particularly innovative you want to tell me about…'

'That's not… God, just for once, can you be serious about this?'

'*Is* it serious? That's sort of what I'm here to ask,' Liam said, his smile vanishing. 'Jenny's worried about Winter. *I'm* worried about Winter. And yes, before you ask, I'm even worried about you. Do you know what you're doing here?'

Josh thought about how Winter had fallen apart in his arms last night. How he'd worshipped every inch of her body, committing it to memory in case it were whipped away from him again without warning.

Did he know what he was doing?

Saying goodbye.

'I'm taking a risk,' he said softly. 'Because honestly, Liam, I don't know what else to do. We've talked and talked this week. We've uncovered a lot of pain, a lot of history, and I think we understand each other better than ever.'

'So you're getting back together?' The astonishment in Liam's voice wasn't entirely encouraging.

'That's not...exactly the plan.' Josh winced as he realised how, in the cold light of day, last night's idea—born out of lust and need and desperation—didn't quite stand up to reality as well as he'd like.

'Then what is?'

'We figured that if talking it all out hadn't helped us move on, maybe we needed another sort of closure.'

Liam's eyebrows hit close to his hairline as

he snorted a laugh. 'This is a "we'll just sleep together once and get it out of our system" plan? Haven't you been in enough romcoms to know that *never* works?'

Josh slumped against the wall. 'The idea was that because things ended so abruptly between us, and because those last six months were so…awful, this was what we hadn't had real closure on. Us being together like this. We hadn't had a chance to say goodbye to us.'

'And now?' Liam asked. 'Do you feel like you can move on now?'

An image of Winter lying in his bed, her black hair against the white sheets, her sated body relaxed and peaceful, burned against the back of his eyes. 'No.'

How could he ever move on from that? From what they were together?

From how in love with her he had always been—and would always be?

Had he just done the one thing that might actually destroy him this time?

He swore, quietly but vehemently, and Liam clapped a hand against his shoulder in sympathy. 'I guess you two have got some talking to do.'

'I guess.' Except Josh didn't want to talk any more. They'd done that, almost to death.

And he didn't want to say goodbye.

So what *did* he want?

He wanted to try again. He wanted to believe that things could be different this time around.

That things could be easy between them this time.

He wanted to remind her how good they'd been, before everything had gone wrong. How good they could be again. To show her that he'd listened, and he'd learned. That they could get it right this time and everything would be plain sailing.

Love would be enough this time around.

Liam was watching him. 'What do you need? How can I help?'

Josh shook his head. 'I think this one needs to be all me.' Then an idea struck him. 'Actually, there is something you could do. Help me find the right place to talk to her.' Because he had a feeling Winter was going to need some convincing.

'Not the penis museum again?' Liam guessed.

'Definitely not the penis museum,' Josh said. 'I was thinking something rather more... romantic.'

'Such as?'

Josh smiled. 'Let me put on some pants and I'll tell you.'

* * *

'Where, exactly, are we going?' Winter asked as Josh bundled her into the car that was waiting for them at the side door the following evening.

'It's a surprise,' Josh said. 'Can't you just trust me?'

'Last time you took me on a surprise date we ended up at the Icelandic Phallological Museum,' Winter pointed out.

'Ah, but this time I didn't let *Liam* come up with the destination,' Josh said.

'I suppose that's something.'

They'd had a blissful couple of days together—mostly staying in Josh's suite or the lagoon, only venturing out for dinner with Liam and Jenny, during which they'd sat on opposite sides of the table and pretended not to be playing footsie underneath.

Winter had also pretended not to notice the scorching looks between Liam and her assistant, because if she started asking all the questions that raised, she was sure they'd have some of their own to ask her and Josh.

Questions she didn't have any answers to. Like what would happen when their Iceland trip was over in less than two days, and they had to return to the real world.

Questions like *What the hell am I doing?*

Objectively, it was hard to see a way that this would end well, when she studied the situation in the cold light of day. They'd already tried marriage once, and failed. She was focused on her career now, and had no interest in trying to live up to Josh's high ideals of what a perfect marriage should be. Plus, she did not want her burgeoning reputation as a director to be buried under other people's interest in her love life. She didn't want to lose herself that way again. So she needed privacy, not internet fame.

Something she'd had to remind Josh when he'd cornered her outside the bathrooms in the restaurant the night before and kissed her breathless. Of course, his solution to that had been to drag her into the unmanned cloakroom nearby and continue kissing her which, while a *lot* of fun, had resulted in them having to leave the space a few minutes apart, and a lot of knowing looks from their friends.

She just hoped the two influencers she'd passed on her way back to the table hadn't noticed her mussed hair and smudged lipstick. Or the dazed look on Josh's face when he'd followed her a couple of minutes later.

But now they were heading somewhere away from everyone else, somewhere Josh had chosen, and she had a feeling he was going to be looking for some of those answers once they arrived.

Maybe she could just distract him with sex. Because she was pretty sure she wasn't ready to deal with the real world again yet.

'This place is incredible.' Winter stared around her at the tiny glass cottage Josh had brought them to, awed by the sheer amount of window between the metal frames and walls. Thank goodness there were no other structures on the horizon, and not another soul around for miles now their driver had left, because a place like this didn't provide much in the way of privacy otherwise.

But as it was…they were in the middle of nowhere, in a glass house with a giant king-sized bed covered in furry blankets and rugs occupying the central space. And Winter was starting to think that maybe Josh hadn't brought her here to talk at all.

'It's the perfect place to view the Northern Lights.' Coming up behind her, Josh wrapped his arms around her middle, pulling her close against his chest. 'I told Liam I wanted something properly romantic this time, somewhere we could relax without worrying about anyone seeing us. And I said I wanted to see the Northern Lights. So he found us this place.'

'It's perfect.' From the wood-burning stove in the corner to the hamper of easy to prepare and eat food in the tiny kitchenette, Winter couldn't imagine a better place to spend their last night together in Iceland.

Even if the lights didn't show, or the clouds covered them, she had a feeling they'd make the most of this place anyway.

Josh had dumped their bags by the entranceway and Winter left them there for now, moving instead to the bed. Flopping down on her back, she propped herself up on her elbows, staring through the glass roof at the sky above.

A moment later Josh joined her—bringing with him a bottle of champagne from the hamper, two glasses and a box of chocolates.

'You really have thought of everything,' she said as he opened the bottle with a pop.

'That's the hope. Because I don't want either of us to have to think about *anything* between now and when that car arrives to take us back to the Ice House Hotel tomorrow morning.' He poured her a glass of champagne and handed it to her, before pouring his own and placing the bottle on the bedside table. 'Sound good?'

'Sounds *perfect*.' Winter took a sip of champagne, letting the bubbles burst pleasurably on her tongue before raising her glass in a toast. 'Here's to escaping reality for a while.'

Josh clinked his glass, then made his own toast. 'Here's to new beginnings.'

Winter felt the first stirrings of doubt start in her stomach, but smiled anyway, drowning her worries in another gulp of champagne.

They were here together, for fun, in this most incredible place. Reality could wait.

CHAPTER ELEVEN

'I'VE NEVER SEEN anything like it,' Winter whispered beside his ear. 'It's so beautiful.'

It was later now, much later, and the Northern Lights had come out to play—something Josh was taking as a sign. This time of year was a good time to see them, but still nothing was guaranteed, and they could have easily disappeared behind cloud cover tonight.

But there they were, glowing and swirling green and white and purple through the glass roof of their tiny home for the night. They felt like a benediction from the universe, a sign that he'd done the right thing bringing Winter here.

That they were doing the right thing, reconnecting this way.

He pulled Winter closer into his arms as they snuggled under the furs and blankets on the bed, staring up through the glass ceiling at the incredible phenomenon overhead.

Not as beautiful as you, he thought, but didn't say.

It was a cliché, like something from one of his movies, and he knew she'd pull a face at the line.

But it was true anyway.

'Good date then?' he asked. 'Better than the penis museum?'

She snorted a laugh at that. 'Different,' she said after a moment. 'The museum was fun. And... I think we needed it, to help us lighten up.'

'Plus you kissed me that night.' Josh smiled at the memory. 'So it can't have been all bad.'

'The waffles were pretty good.' He poked her in the side, and she laughed. 'No, it wasn't bad at all. I... I just liked spending time with you again.'

'Me too.'

They'd done a lot more than just spend time together now. More than just kiss too. In some ways it felt as if they'd fallen straight back into the fairy tale that had been derailed by Winter's miscarriage, and the collapse of their marriage that had followed.

And Josh had to admit he was starting to hope again. He knew what he'd done wrong now. Maybe he could get it right this time around.

If she let him.

If she didn't... His heart stung at the thought.

In the corner the wood-burning stove crackled and popped as it warmed the room, also providing the only light beside the glowing rivers in the sky. The remains of the picnic dinner they'd shared sat on the table beside it, along with the empty bottle of champagne.

Josh couldn't think of anywhere in the world he'd rather be.

'This is the perfect way to spend our last night in Iceland,' Winter said, snuggling closer again, and Josh felt the first pinprick in his dream.

He didn't want to ask. He wanted to just fall back into this life and have it all back again.

But he knew he couldn't just assume that was what happened next. Assuming that just because he was happy meant that she was too had been part of what had broken them last time.

He couldn't make that mistake again.

'What about when we leave Iceland?' he asked tentatively. 'Do you think we might have this again, somewhere else?'

She lifted her head from his chest and gave him a curious look. 'Well, there are other places you can see the Northern Lights, I suppose.'

'That's not what I meant.'

Her bare skin was pressed so closely to his that Josh felt the tension enter her body. 'What *did* you mean?'

'I mean…we're leaving Iceland tomorrow. We've talked, I think, about everything we needed to talk about to find some closure on everything that happened. And we've, well…'

'Found physical closure as well?' Winter suggested, with eyebrows arched.

'That's one way of putting it.' She moved against his body and he could feel it reacting to her closeness again, threatening to distract him away from the conversation they needed to have. But he couldn't bring himself to stop her.

'So, what's the problem?' She pressed a kiss to his collarbone and he shivered.

'I'm not ready to say goodbye again.'

It was, he'd realised, somewhere around the time the skies started dancing above them, as simple and as complicated as that. And he couldn't leave this place without knowing if she was on the same page.

Winter sat up, folding her legs underneath her and pulling a blanket around her—for warmth or because she didn't want to have this conversation naked, Josh wasn't entirely sure.

'What are you suggesting, exactly?'

He forced himself into a sitting position too, leaning against the wooden headboard with a pillow at his back.

'I don't know, exactly,' he said with a sigh. 'That depends where your head is with this too. I just… Being with you again this week has reminded me how great it was when we were together—'

'It wasn't all great,' Winter reminded him sharply. 'That's one of the reasons I left.'

'I know. I know that. But…we're older and wiser now, right? Don't you think there's a chance we could get it right this time?' There had to be, surely? Otherwise, what were they even doing here together?

Winter pulled back a little further. She couldn't go far on the bed, but Josh still felt the distance between them like an icy blast of Icelandic air.

'I can't go back to being the woman I was when I married you.' The words were stark, but the look of horror in Winter's eyes was even starker.

'I don't want that,' he reassured her. 'Neither of us are the people we were then, and that's *good*. We've grown. But I want more time with the Winter I've got to know here, this week. The woman you are *now*.'

Some of the tension disappeared from Winter's shoulders, bare above the blanket. But not all. The wariness around her eyes remained too.

'So you're thinking we…date?'

'Maybe? I mean, we're a bit past that in some ways. But in others…' He thought about their date at the penis museum, and how fun it had been to just hang out together. 'You know, dating could be fun.'

Winter's small smile made him think she was remembering the same things. 'I suppose it could.' Then the smile fell away. 'Except… we were able to do this, here, because we had Liam to help us sneak around, and book places out so we had total privacy. How are you expecting us to manage that back in the real world? Especially with us both working away so much.'

Josh slumped a little against the headboard. 'You don't want anyone to know about us.'

'I thought…' A frown line formed between her eyebrows. 'I thought we talked about that. I don't want the only thing anyone knows about me to be that I'm dating you—again. I don't want to be the subject of gossip and world expectations. Plus… I mean…it ended badly before. If that's going to happen again, I'd rather do it without an audience.'

'Privacy takes the pressure off,' Josh said, musing. 'I guess I can see that.'

'If we're really going to try this, it needs to be just between us,' Winter pressed. 'That's the only way I can handle it.'

He pushed aside his first, instinctive feeling—that she was ashamed or embarrassed by their relationship—and focused in on what she was really saying.

She was scared. He could see it now, in the shadows in her eyes. And he could understand it too—hell, he was petrified himself.

Last time around, they'd both been swept away by the romance of it all. By the fairy tale.

This time, they both knew exactly how badly they could hurt each other. How, if this fell apart again, it could destroy them. They'd be fools *not* to be afraid.

But all the same…he couldn't not try.

'Just between us,' he promised. 'We just… try. Okay?'

There was still some uncertainty in Winter's gaze as she nodded. 'Okay.'

He smiled, and hoped it was reassuring. Then he took her into his arms and they lay back and watched the night sky dance above them until they fell asleep.

The plane back to London was packed, and Winter was glad of their first-class tickets. Not least because the Saga Lounge at Reykjavik-Keflavik Airport had given her and Josh the privacy they'd needed to say goodbye.

That had been harder than she'd anticipated. Yes, the last week had been special, and she'd loved being with him again in so many ways. But she'd built her own life away from him over the past five years. She wasn't his doting fairy tale princess any longer, and she wouldn't wither away during their separation.

She wasn't that woman any more. That young, naive, hopeful Winter. She couldn't be. It hurt too much when that hope was broken.

So on the drive back to Liam's hotel from their tiny glass cottage under the Northern Lights, they'd hammered out some rules for their fledging... Winter hesitated to call it a relationship.

Arrangement. That was what it was.

A mutually satisfying arrangement that gave them both the benefits of the relationship they used to have—basically sex and each other's company—without all the issues that had driven them apart. Like the way she lost herself, disappeared into his shadow the moment they were a couple, and how he wanted the picket fence perfect life, when that was *not* something she could give him.

Even the separations caused by work that had been a problem for their marriage were now just something factored into their arrangement.

It was all going to be fine.

And there was absolutely no reason for her to miss him before the plane had even left the runway.

Jenny, meanwhile, looked like there was definitely something she was regretting leaving behind. And she had been spending an awful lot of time with Liam…

'So,' Winter said, twisting slightly in her seat to face her assistant, who was staring out of the opposite window. 'How was *your* stay in Iceland? Anything…new and interesting happen there?'

Jenny turned to face her, eyebrows raised. 'Are we really going to talk about *my* sex life, when you just shared the most passionate goodbye kiss in the history of kisses in the airport lounge, with your *ex-husband*?'

'It wasn't *that* passionate,' Winter mumbled, hiding her smile by looking down at her hands.

'It really was,' Jenny assured her. 'Seriously, what's going on there? Liam and I came up with all sorts of theories, but—'

'Liam and you? Because you two were spending so much time together....?'

'Not talking about me right now.' Jenny's gaze turned serious, and Winter swallowed as she met it. 'Winter. As your friend—a friend who remembers what happened last time you and Josh were together, incidentally—I'm asking. What's going on, and are you sure about it?'

'We have an agreement,' Winter said. 'An arrangement. It's going to be fine.'

'An arrangement?'

'Yeah. We set ground rules and everything. Number one: nobody finds out.'

'Well, that sounds like a perfectly sound basis for a loving relationship.' The sarcasm rang out from Jenny's voice.

'Which is why it's an arrangement, not a relationship,' Winter shot back. 'We've done the whole fairy tale thing, and I have no interest in doing it again. We enjoyed spending time together this week, and we'd like to keep doing so, when our schedules permit. But that's it. No big romance, no public hand-holding, no promises I can't keep, or anything like that.'

'Promises you can't keep?' Jenny frowned. 'What do you mean?'

Frustrated, Winter turned to look out of the window. 'It doesn't matter. I didn't mean to say that.'

'But you *did* say it. Which means you're thinking it. What promises, Winter?' Jenny sighed. 'You know how this goes when you bottle stuff like this up. Neither of us wants to go back there, do we?'

Winter thought of those horrible days and weeks and months after she'd lost the baby. After she'd left Josh. When all she had was Jenny's spare room and the pain of her memories.

'No,' she admitted.

'Which is why I'm the person you tell,' Jenny said. 'No one else in the world needs to know, but you need to tell someone, and that person is me.'

'I don't pay you enough for this,' Winter stalled.

'I do my job for the money. This I do because you're family, and I know you'd do the same for me.'

That much was true, Winter supposed.

Which meant she was going to have to ask a lot more questions about Liam later. But for now...

'He still wants that picket fence life,' she said with a sigh. 'He says he's moved on, but I *know* him, Jen. He wants the perfect romance, the perfect wife, the perfect kids...and I can't give him that. I just can't.'

Jenny's eyes were sympathetic. 'Well, there's *perfect* perfect, and then there's perfect for him. Maybe he's more interested in the second one these days?'

'I don't think so.' Josh's world view was ingrained in him, by the perfect marriage his parents had shared before his father's death, not to mention his brother's own ideal relationship. 'He might *say* he doesn't need those things, but I know that the day will come when he'll realise he's not complete or happy without it. And I can't face losing him again then.'

'You've changed a lot in the last five years,' Jenny pointed out. 'Maybe Josh has too.'

Winter's heart lurched—was it with hope, or just turbulence?

But she shook her head. 'I can't risk that. Not again.'

Which was why they had to stick to the arrangement. It was the only way she could see she had of getting out of this with her heart intact.

The flat Josh had leased in LA, ready for his next shoot, seemed stark and empty which, considering the only other place he'd spent time recently was in a pared back, Scandi-style hotel room with only the bare essentials of his belongings with him, was ridiculous.

Except he knew what that feeling really meant was that Winter wasn't there with him.

Throwing his keys into the bowl on the kitchen counter, he hung up his jacket, grabbed his phone from his pocket and dropped onto the leather couch to call her.

The eight-hour time difference between LA and London, plus their differing work schedules, had made keeping in touch trickier than he'd like, but they'd managed so far. Over the week since they'd left Iceland, they'd spoken by video call most days, and at least messaged on the days where that wasn't possible.

'Hey,' he said when her face appeared on the screen. 'How're things there?'

'Mmm...fine,' she said. 'You're done early?'

Josh looked out of his window at the Californian afternoon. 'Started in the middle of the night,' he said. 'My call was stupid o'clock this morning, but at least it means I'm done in time to call you before you turn in for the night.'

'Only just.' On the screen, Winter's smile was tired. 'It's been a long day here too.'

'But you're still coming out here next weekend?' He didn't mean to sound quite as eager as he did but, well, he'd missed her.

Not that he planned on telling her that just yet. Winter still seemed skittish whenever they spoke about what happened next between them, so Josh was trying to learn to go with the flow and take each day as it came.

He supposed he could understand her reluctance to plan too far ahead. Last time they'd tried this they'd been engaged within six months, married in under a year, and with their whole lives together planned out over late-night conversations and whispered dreams.

And it had all gone to hell. This time, he was happy to move a little slower if it still got him where he wanted to be—with her.

'I'm still coming,' Winter assured him. 'I mean, I kind of need to be there for the awards ceremony anyway, right?'

The awards ceremony they would both be attending—separately. Another thing Josh was willing to live with as long as he got to take her home to bed afterwards, once the cameras and the press weren't watching.

It wouldn't be for ever, he reassured himself. They were just going under the radar for now so they could take the time to figure out things between themselves. That was all.

One day he'd be able to walk out there with Winter on his arm again, the proudest man in Hollywood.

Just not yet.

'I'm not ready,' Winter had said apologetically, when he'd asked about attending the awards together on one late-night phone call. *'You know that appearing at something like that together would be tantamount to announcing our second engagement. The gossip sites would have us married before the winners were announced. And that's not... I can't do that.'*

She was right, he knew. Going public would push them to define exactly what was happening between them before they'd had a chance to figure it out themselves.

It didn't mean he liked the idea of hiding their relationship away any better, though.

'You'll come here before the awards, though?' He needed time alone with her before he had to pretend to be nothing more than her ex-husband in public.

'I will,' she promised. 'You'll see me before the awards. I'm hoping I can come out a few days early and we'll have some time together first.'

The tight fist that had been forming around his heart loosened a bit. She wasn't pulling away, wasn't leaving him again now that they'd left the magical bubble Iceland had given them. She was just being cautious. Protecting their privacy.

He could live with that. For now.

'That would be nice,' he said, trying to keep things light. 'And we won't need to worry about bumping into any paparazzi types if we just stay in bed all week…'

Winter laughed at that, helping his spirits rise a little more. 'That's a plan I can live with,' she agreed. 'I'll let you know my travel plans as soon as I—' She broke off as a chime sounded from her computer.

'What is it?' Josh asked.

'Check your notifications.' Winter's voice was tight.

Josh swiped away from the active call and opened up his Instagram account, where his notifications were flashing. Since he kept them pared down to the bare minimum, that meant *something* had to have happened.

'Got it?' Winter asked.

His heart was racing in his chest, the terrible feeling of doom chasing him as he swiped through the app.

'Almost—' And then, there it was.

A photo of the two of them in the apparently not so private lagoon at Liam's hotel, their arms wrapped around each other, their faces clearly visible. And the next frame, showing them kissing. From the grainy nature of the shots, it looked as if the photographer had zoomed in a lot.

Just checking through my photos from my amazing trip to Iceland and look what I spotted in the background of these landscape shots? Are Hollywood's favourite fairy tale couple back on again?

CHAPTER TWELVE

WINTER COULD FEEL the panic rising inside her the longer she stared at the photo on her screen. She needed Jenny here to help make sense of this, to strategise and decide on their next moves. Her phone was beeping with another call coming through from her agent, but she couldn't take that yet. Not until she knew what she was going to say.

And not while Josh was still on the line, swearing like a sailor as he saw the same images she had.

There was no denying it was them in the photo. Their presence in Iceland had been well publicised by Liam's team at the hotel, and they had both posted their own social media photos of the trip too—taking care that none of the shots included each other. They'd been *so* careful the whole time. And now this.

Her hand shook as she banished the images and returned to Josh's face on the other end of the video call.

'What do you want to do?' His expression was more serious than she was used to seeing from him, especially recently. She knew he was putting the ball in her court, that he'd go along with whatever she needed, because that was the sort of man he was. And she loved him for it. Had loved him when she'd married him and loved him now. She wasn't even sure if she'd ever really stopped loving him at any time in between.

But love, as her failed marriage and broken body had proved, wasn't always enough.

Love hadn't kept her baby alive inside her. It hadn't protected her from the sickness that had racked her body before that. And it hadn't stopped her walking away when she knew that staying in that marriage would destroy her.

Worse still, she knew that love would be no protection at all against the camera flashes and the social media chaos that would follow now. Those photos were out there, and the world was watching—just when she'd hoped that they would avert their gaze.

She could already feel her sense of self slipping. Backsliding into the woman she'd been, rather than the one she'd worked so hard to become. She'd thought she'd finished that process—had rebuilt herself from the ground up into someone strong enough to hold her own in front of anything. That she could be her new self and keep Josh at the distance she needed, and have both the things her heart desired—Josh, and the new life she'd built for herself.

But she knew now that new life would buckle. It wasn't strong enough. *She* wasn't strong enough.

Already, the same feeling of panic she'd experienced so often in those months after she'd left Josh was rising again. Already she was starting to doubt herself.

What had she been thinking, imagining that things would be different this time? Even if Josh really had changed—if he'd reassessed what he wanted from life and from her, if he was willing to do things her way this time, to let her set the pace and keep their relationship in the dark…the world wasn't going to let this be enough.

Her love life was going to be thrust back into the spotlight whether she liked it or not. And whether she and Josh were back together again was the only thing people were going to be talking about across the country—heck, across the world!

The film she'd worked so hard for, the new career she'd built for herself, the whole *life* she'd recreated from the ashes of tragedy... they were going to be swept away. Because the only thing that mattered to the press was who she was sleeping with.

I'm not ready for this. I can't handle this.

She had to set her boundaries to ensure that *she* remembered what mattered about herself, even if no one else did.

She'd almost broken under the intense scrutiny the media had placed on her marriage, miscarriage and divorce. She couldn't go through all that again. And she knew that, if she tried, it would probably spell the end of any relationship she and Josh managed to salvage anyway.

But she also knew Josh would want to try. He'd need to believe that she didn't want this, didn't want any real relationship between them, if he were ever to step away.

'We need to deny it,' she said before her heart could overrule her head. 'We need to put out a statement making it categorically clear that while we remain friends after our divorce, that's all.'

Josh's usually mobile face stilled. 'But it's not.'

Winter shook her head. 'I'm not ready for that information to be out there yet.'

'But if it comes out later, everyone will

know we lied,' Josh said. Winter winced, and he continued, 'Unless you're not planning to *ever* tell people we're back together.'

Back together.

Was that what they were? Already he'd made this into something more than she'd agreed to. She'd agreed to a fling in Iceland, to find that physical closure as well as the emotional one. And okay, she'd sort of said yes to carrying on when they could…but the arrangement she'd agreed to didn't add up to a relationship. It didn't mean 'back together'. Did it?

Clearly in Josh's head it did.

He'd promised he didn't want the things she couldn't give him—that picket fence life with the kids in the yard and her at home waiting for him. But he was already trying to make it happen.

She could feel the walls closing in on her again. The panic rising in her chest.

She'd told him all this. But it seemed it hadn't sunk in.

And now… She couldn't have this argument now. She needed to get off the phone, find a way to breathe again, and fix this.

'I can't talk about this right now,' Winter said. 'I just… It's so soon. And there's so much going on.' She cast around for an excuse that he'd buy. Something that would make him back off, for now, at least.

Something that wasn't *I can't be what you need me to be*. Because he still didn't seem to believe that, even though she'd proven it time and again. Was proving it right now, for that matter.

'I don't want news stories about you and me to overshadow the awards next weekend,' she said, hating herself even as she spoke. 'That wouldn't be fair to everyone who worked so hard on the movie, would it?'

'I… I guess not,' Josh said haltingly.

'So it's probably best if I don't come see you before the show, under the circumstances.' If she saw him she'd break. If he kissed her, held her, he'd know she was lying. That this wasn't about the film at all.

She loved him. She wanted him. But she couldn't be what he needed. She'd fail him again and she wouldn't survive the heartbreak this time around. Maybe he wouldn't either.

They both loved too deeply to say goodbye.

'If that's what you really want.' His voice was cold now.

'It is,' she lied.

'Then I guess I'll see you on the red carpet.' He ended the call with a sharp tap and Winter stared at the blank screen for long minutes afterwards, but the tears just wouldn't come.

She'd done what she needed to do, to protect them both. What was the point of crying now?

Josh stared at his phone, wondering what the hell had just happened.

How had they gone from planning to spend three days in bed to not even seeing each other at all, in the space of a couple of minutes?

Blinking at the screen, he pulled up the fuzzy photos of them together in Iceland again. The comments were mounting up underneath them, some enthusiastic and hopeful, some disdainful, mostly accusing Winter of wanting her cake and eating it.

In fact, reading the vitriol some of his fans shot in his ex-wife's direction, he could completely understand why she might not want their reunion to be public knowledge yet. Hell, he *had* understood. That was why he'd agreed to all the secrecy in the first place.

But now the news was out there…

He'd known she wanted to protect their privacy while they figured out where things were going. But he'd never foreseen that she'd call the whole thing off if they got found out.

He was missing something here. And he had no idea what it was.

Unless…

A new comment on the post of the travel blogger who'd been with them in Iceland caught his eye.

She's just leading him on again. Just you watch. She'll be using this to promote that movie of hers before you know it.

Was that it? Was this *really* all about the movie nomination somehow? Except Winter had said she didn't want them to distract from that. And besides, he *knew* her. She wouldn't use him that way.

Another comment read:

I can't believe he's going to let her break his heart again. She was never good enough for him.

Except he knew the opposite was true, there. *He* hadn't been good enough for *her*.

He kept scanning down the comments, unable to stop himself, even though he knew that none of these people really knew anything about him or Winter, or what they'd shared in Iceland.

They'd all formed an opinion, though. Just

like they had after Winter had left him, five years ago.

The comments in the media and online then had been vicious, especially before the news of the miscarriage had come out. Winter had wanted to keep everything private, of course—so had he, for that matter. But it hadn't made any difference. Someone always talked.

But the rumours that made it out there were given the same weighting as the facts, and their fans picked and chose the ones that best suited the narrative they wanted to tell. His fans painted Winter as a callous heartbreaker. Hers blamed him for not being supportive enough.

The worst of the commentary had definitely been pointed at Winter, though. He'd seen that, even then, through his anger and his pain after she'd left.

No wonder she didn't want to go through all that again.

She wouldn't have to if we just stayed together this time.

The thought nagged in his head. Was this reluctance to admit their relationship because she *didn't* see it lasting this time?

He hadn't seen the end coming last time,

although she clearly had. Was history repeating itself?

There were dozens more comments already, and notifications pinging into his email about other mentions of the story across the internet. This was going to be everywhere, fast.

With a sigh, Josh tapped to read a message from his agent that read:

CALL ME!

He supposed he should do just that.

If Winter wanted damage limitation measures, that was what he'd give her. But he suspected the damage to his heart was already done.

Maybe she'd been right all along. They'd failed at marriage once. Why would they do any better this time, when they couldn't even make it two weeks into a new relationship without a crisis?

Better to end it now with a bruised heart than later with a smashed one.

Perhaps this was the closure he'd really been looking for in Iceland. The final death knell of the fairy tale of Josh and Winter. The one that would let him move on and find the sort of relationship he'd always wanted. One like his parents had shared.

Really, this could be a good thing. In the end.

He just wished that closure didn't hurt so damn much.

'I just don't understand,' Jenny said, staring at the fuzzy photos on the computer screen.

'Neither do I,' Winter grumbled. 'Liam *said* that the lagoon was private.'

Jenny shot her a look Winter couldn't quite read. 'That's not what I meant.'

'So what *did* you mean?' She wasn't up to inference today.

'I thought you and Josh were happy again. You certainly looked it when you got back from your mysterious Northern Lights trip.'

'We were,' Winter said, mystified. What did happy have to do with anything here? 'I mean, we had a nice time together.'

'So why am I proofreading a press release denying that there's anything going on between the two of you?' Jenny put the paper in her hand down and met Winter's gaze across the desk.

Winter looked away. 'Because there isn't. There can't be.'

'Why not?'

Standing up, Winter paced across the lounge of her London flat towards the darkened window. It was so late already, but she couldn't sleep until they'd sorted this. 'I need to focus on the movie right now. And the next one—on my career. I don't have time for love.'

'Then what was Iceland?' Jenny pressed.

'A goodbye.' The lie stung even to speak it. She'd thought, just for a moment as the Northern Lights had danced overhead, that it could be a beginning. It had all seemed possible then.

It didn't now.

'Really? That's not what it looked like at the airport.' Jenny pulled a face. 'Well, it kind of did, because you *were* actually saying goodbye. But you know what I mean. It didn't look like goodbye *for ever.*'

'We both agreed we wanted closure on how our marriage ended,' Winter said, trying to sound pragmatic. 'For a while, I thought maybe we could carry on with something else. But these photos have made clear to me that is not possible.'

Jenny sighed, and reached across the desk to take Winter's hand. 'You're not talking to the press now, Winter. This is me. You know I understand how scary this must before for you. So tell me. What's going on in your head? Is this *really* all about the movie, or the award, or your career?'

'Why wouldn't it be?'

'Because I've never seen you look at another person the way you look at Josh. And I don't think you'll ever even want to, will you?'

Jenny's words slashed deep towards her heart, but they couldn't reach it. Winter had put back those walls that had defended her so well after her divorce, the ones that wouldn't let in the awful words and comments about her on the internet, or the prime-time gossip shows debating whether she had ever actually been pregnant at all.

She wasn't going to do any of that again. She wouldn't let it hurt her.

And if that meant keeping her friends out as well as her enemies, so be it.

Except apparently Jenny didn't get the memo.

'Winter. What are you doing?' Jenny's voice had dropped to a whisper. '*Why* are you doing it? I don't believe this is about a movie, or an award. I don't even really think it's about your career.'

'Why shouldn't it be?' Winter shot back. 'You know how horrific this job can be to women—you've lived it. You know how unfair they are when it comes to things like this. My whole life will be picked apart, and that's all anyone will care about. Not the work I've done, or all the other people who've invested so much of themselves in our movie. No one will even remember the *name* of the film, just that I tried to seduce my ex-husband in a geothermal lagoon!'

She was shouting, Winter realised. And standing up. She didn't remember doing either of those things.

Maybe she wasn't handling this as calmly as she'd hoped.

'You're not wrong,' Jenny said softly, and Winter knew she was remembering how she'd come to work for her in the first place, and regretted reminding her of it. 'I know all that better than almost anyone. But I don't think that would be enough to stop *you*. Not if this is love.'

'Love?' Winter shook her head. 'Do you really think that's enough? Even after everything you've seen in this place? Everything you've been through? You think love can fix it all?'

'Not fix it,' Jenny said, meeting her gaze steadily. 'But you know that the gossip sites will talk about you anyway—that's part of the gig. Love—being with someone who truly knows and understands you—I can only imagine that's what would make the rest of it bearable.'

The worst thing was, Winter knew that she was right. It just didn't change anything.

'I can't, Jenny. I can't love him again.'

'Why not?'

'Because…' Winter took a breath. 'He wants things I can't give him, remember? Marriage and kids and a perfect wife and I'm *not* perfect and he knows it.'

'You're scared of getting pregnant again,' Jenny guessed, and there was something that flashed behind her eyes that Winter couldn't quite read.

'I'm terrified of it all.' It felt good to admit it. 'Yes, the idea of getting pregnant and that sick again is awful, but nowhere near as horrific as the thought of losing another baby. And it's not just that! If I can't give Josh the family he wants, what *can* I give him? Eventually he'll want more and I'll lose him too, and I just can't take that again. I *can't*.'

'I get that. You're too scared to take a second chance on love,' Jenny said. 'Oh, Winter.'

'I can't do it, Jenny. I won't let him down that way. And I won't risk my heart that way either.'

Jenny's gaze was direct, demanding, and the grip on her hand had grown tighter. 'But what's the alternative?'

'I carry on the way I have been for the last five years.' Winter attempted a casual shrug and a watery smile. 'I focus on my career. I make great movies and maybe even win an award.'

'That's it?' Jenny asked. 'That's the plan?' She sounded disappointed. Like she'd thought there would be something more. Some great wisdom to make sense of it all.

'It's all I've got,' Winter told her.

And she hoped against all hope that it was going to be enough.

CHAPTER THIRTEEN

JOSH DIDN'T ANSWER the first knock on the door of his house. Or the second.

In fact, it wasn't until Liam called him and said, 'Open the door and let me in, you tosser!' before hanging up that he dragged himself off the couch at all.

'What are you doing in LA?' Josh let Liam in and slammed the door behind him, hoping that no lingering paparazzi had caught the ex-Hollywood heartthrob showing up on his doorstep with a bottle of bourbon in the middle of the afternoon, just three days after his ex-wife had issued a statement categorically denying any rekindling of their relationship. It wouldn't take a genius to ferret out the subtext there.

'Just a stopover.' Liam headed straight for the kitchen and pulled out two cut glass tumblers. 'I'm on my way to Costa Rica to my latest hotel site. Thought I might drop in on an old friend.'

'Let me guess. Jenny was busy?' He'd seen the looks between the two of them and, as good a friend as Liam was, Josh couldn't believe he'd really come all this way to salve his broken heart.

Liam paused in pouring the bourbon. 'I didn't come to see Jenny. She's still in London with Winter anyway. I came here because... I feel like this is my fault.'

'You came here for absolution?'

'That's why I brought bourbon.' Liam handed him one of the glasses and took the other.

Josh dropped onto the couch at the far end of the kitchen, motioning for Liam to follow him.

'It's not your fault,' Josh told him. 'You brought us together again, sure. But that had to happen some time. You just gave us space to do it in private.'

'Apart from the Instagram snappers.' Liam sipped his drink. 'I *am* sorry about them. And I genuinely wasn't trying to get you two back together, you know.'

'Really?' Josh asked, sceptical. 'What *were*

you trying to do then? Distract us so you could seduce Jenny without Winter objecting?'

Liam waved a hand at him. 'None of it had anything to do with Jenny, okay?'

'Then what?'

'Is it so hard to believe I just wanted the two of you to be friends again? To stop living with this huge tragedy hanging over you, and never moving on?' Liam leaned forward, his forearms resting on his knees, and surveyed Josh with serious eyes. 'Mate, I know what it's like to live in the past. I know I'm every bit as guilty of it as you. And I know how bloody hard it is to put the events that define who we are as a person behind us and move on. I'm trying—damned if I know if I'm succeeding, but I'm trying. But you... you wouldn't even admit you were stuck back there, mentally living in a fairy tale that ended years ago.'

'Believe me, I know my marriage ended,' Josh said caustically. 'And I knew it *before* my ex-wife took my heart and trampled on it again.'

Liam winced. 'Maybe you knew it, but you hadn't moved on from it, had you? I mean, seriously. Have you had anything past a third date in five years?'

'I was working,' Josh pointed out. 'A lot. Hardly conducive to starting a new love affair.'

'Really?' Liam raised his eyebrows. 'Half the Hollywood relationships we know started on film sets. *Including* yours and Winter's.'

'And look how *that* worked out.' Josh sighed. 'I know what you were trying to do, Liam. Give us closure. Right?'

'I guess that's as good a word for it as any.' Liam sat back, sprawled against the soft sofa cushions, his eyes contemplative. 'It's hard to find that closure sometimes—especially when the person you need it from is gone. I figured at least you and Winter were both still alive to find it. I just didn't expect—' He broke off.

'What? That we'd fall into bed together again?' Josh asked bitterly. 'Trust me, neither did I.'

Liam gave a soft chuckle. 'Honestly? I wasn't counting on it or anything, but with you two…the way you fell for each other the first time, that was something else. And I've never seen two people look at each other with such love as you guys did on your wedding day. So, yeah, I guess I always figured there was a chance you two would get back together again.' He met Josh's gaze and held it with an intensity that was almost unsettling. 'I just didn't think you'd be such idiots as to throw away that kind of love a second time, when some of us would kill for a second chance like that.'

A shard of guilt stabbed Josh somewhere around his heart, as he remembered how much his friend had lost. But still he shook his head.

'I didn't throw it away. She did.'

'What do you mean?'

Josh explained, as best he could, everything that had led them to this moment. How he'd thought they were trying again, for real and for ever. But she'd chosen her career and her privacy over him.

'I guess she never really saw us going the distance,' he said. 'Or else she'd never have given up so easily on us. But really, it's probably for the best.'

'The best?' Liam asked. 'How do you figure that?'

Josh had spent the last few days, ever since that picture leaked, looking at the situation from every angle, and had finally landed on one he could live with.

'Love—real love—it's not meant to be this hard, right?'

Liam laughed. 'In my experience, love is the hardest thing of all.'

'But it *shouldn't* be, that's what I'm saying. True love is meant to be effortless. Like you couldn't imagine being apart. That's what it was like when Winter and I met. Falling in love with her was the easiest thing I ever did.'

'Until things got hard.'

'Exactly!'

'Do you really believe that?' Liam asked, looking amused. 'I mean, have you just made so many romcoms now that you've bought into the idea of the eternal happy ending? That once you reach the last frame it's all sunshine and strawberries from there on out?'

'It's not the movies that taught me that,' Josh hit back. 'I've seen it. Remember? My mom and dad, they had it. Graham and Ashley, they have the same. It's not *work* for them, being in love. It's not this…this pain and frustration and feeling of loss and lack of understanding. If anything, it's the opposite.'

Liam eyed him for a moment, then drained the rest of the bourbon from his glass before standing up. 'Well. If you're determined to give up on the love of your life just because things got hard, and you believe love is meant to be easy...' He shook his head and placed the empty glass on the kitchen counter. 'Then there's nothing more I can say. Except...call your brother.'

Josh frowned. 'What?'

'Call Graham and ask him to confirm your theory. That true love is easy. That's all I ask.' Liam grabbed his jacket from where he'd draped it over the back of a kitchen stool and shot Josh a grin. 'And let me know how it goes, yeah? I've got to move. Costa Rica beckons.'

He walked out of the door with a backward wave, leaving Josh wondering exactly what Liam thought Graham knew that he didn't.

Winter reached for the water glass on the table between her and Melody, the star of *Another Time and Place*, and tried to stifle a sigh. This pre-awards press junket seemed to be going on for ever, and the hotel suite they'd been given for meeting the journalists was stifling. Plus, apparently their next—and final—interviewer of the day was running late, interviewing someone else in another suite.

'Bored of talking about the movie already?' Melody asked, her perfect eyebrows arched.

'If only they'd *ask* about the movie,' Winter said. 'I'll talk about our film and its message all day long. But the first question everyone asks is always about—' She broke off, not wanting to say his name.

'Your ex-husband,' Melody finished for her. 'I read the stories, of course. But I have to admit, none of it really made any sense to me.'

'You and me both,' Winter said with a wry smile. 'I issued a statement when the photos were released. I don't know why people are still going on about it.'

'Because you're the fairy tale, of course,' Melody said with an elegant shrug. 'Everyone loves a fairy tale.'

'We *were* the fairy tale, the better part of ten years ago,' Winter replied. 'And then we were just a failing married couple, then a pair of divorcees. Plenty of those to go around without talking about us.'

'I didn't mean back then, when you first met.' Melody waved a dismissive hand. 'I've seen the photos and all that. You were both very young and beautiful and in love. All very nice. But *now. Now* you're the real thing.'

Winter stared at her in astonishment. 'What on earth do you mean?'

She and Josh were nothing now, and never would be again. She'd seen to that. So why were people still talking about them?

'Young couples falling in love are ten a penny. But you two…finding your way back to each other after heartbreak, taking a second chance on love, even knowing the risks… now *that's* a story worth following.' Melody gave her a wolfish smile. 'You *literally* made the movie about this, Winter. Are you honestly surprised that people are fishing for the story that links your *award-nominated* movie with your real life?'

'I hadn't thought of it like that,' Winter admitted. 'And anyway it isn't really. Like I said, nothing is happening between me and Josh any more. We wanted closure on our relationship and we found it. Now we can move on.'

Melody's gaze was sceptical. 'I think that, if that were true, you wouldn't mind so many questions being asked about him.'

Jumping to her feet, Winter paced to the window, glass of water still in hand. 'It didn't…it didn't end as cleanly as I'd like, that's all. It's an awkward situation.'

'Because he's still in love with you,' Melody guessed.

Winter scoffed. 'If he was, I dare say he isn't any more.' She'd burned that bridge. And she was living with it.

Everything was fine.

Apart from the way her chest ached every time someone said his name.

Melody didn't answer, and when Winter turned to look she found the older actress watching her with compassion in her eyes.

'What?'

Melody shook her head sadly. 'I just think it's a shame. When I made this movie, I hoped it would help *me* move on. To find closure on the love I let go, because I believed I couldn't have this career I wanted so badly *and* a healthy marriage and home. I thought I had to choose, so I did.'

'What happened?' Winter asked.

'I've regretted it every day since,' Melody answered simply. 'I let her go and she found love elsewhere, and I tried to be happy for her...but I never stopped regretting it.'

'I'm sorry.' Winter tried to imagine seeing Josh happy with someone else, but the pain in her chest got worse, so she shook the image away.

She'd seen a few photos of him on dates, or with co-stars, in the years since their divorce. But he'd never seemed to settle down with anyone longer than a few dates. She'd never really been confronted with the idea of him being happy with someone else, except in her imagination.

But that would change now, she realised suddenly. He'd found the closure on their relationship that he'd needed to move on. And while he might be hurt right now that she'd ended things again, he wouldn't take so long to recover this time, she was sure.

Josh still wanted that perfect love— marriage, family, home—the American ideal of a relationship that his parents and brother had. Now she'd made it completely clear that she couldn't give him that, he'd find it with someone else.

He'd fall in love again, with someone who wasn't her.

'You're imagining it, aren't you?' Melody said. 'Your Josh loving someone else.'

'No,' Winter lied. 'He's not my Josh.'

Melody laughed. 'Trust me. However much you're imagining it hurting right now, it's a thousand times worse when it happens in reality.'

Winter swallowed, desperately wishing the images away. But they wouldn't budge.

In her imagination, Josh's new love was tall, willowy, blonde—all the things she wasn't. And pregnant, of course. Of course.

'It doesn't make any difference.' Winter stared out of the window at the LA skyline rather than risk Melody's knowing eyes again. Her whole body felt wrung-out—exhausted and aching. She blamed it on the jet lag, even though she knew she'd felt like this long before she'd left London.

Jenny said she was heartsick. Winter kept ignoring her.

'Why? Why doesn't it make a difference?' Melody asked.

'Because…because I already broke things off. I told him I couldn't do this. I've broken his heart too many times already for him to risk it again on me.'

'Isn't that a decision for him to make?' There was a rustle of fabric as Melody stood up and crossed to stand beside her at the window.

'He wouldn't make it,' Winter said softly. 'That's why I had to do it for him. I can't be what he needs.'

'One thing I've learned, growing older,'

Melody said, 'is that we can't decide what matters for anyone other than ourselves. We can't choose for other people, that's not our right. If you want to be apart from Josh, if you want to watch him find love with someone else, then that's your choice to make. But if the idea makes you want to scream…well. You're choosing it for him, and that's *not* your job.'

Winter swallowed, blinking away the pin-pricks behind her eyes as the tears formed.

'But what if it doesn't work? What if I'm not enough, again?'

And wasn't that what it all came down to? Jenny had told her she was afraid, and she was right.

She was terrified she wouldn't be enough for Josh. That she wouldn't be able to be what he needed. That she'd run again when things got too hard, rather than having those impossible conversations where nobody ever, ever won.

That her heart would break again, whatever decision she made.

'That's the risk you take with love,' Melody said softly, sadly even. 'I'm not saying it's not a big one. But Winter, isn't this the story you were trying to tell the world with our movie? That sometimes the bigger the risk the bigger the reward? That even if you've been hurt, if you've experienced more of life's ups and downs, if you know how bad things can be… you still have to get out there and live.'

'I suppose.' Winter knew Melody was right. But it was so much easier to believe those things when the only heart that might get broken was a fictional one. 'But what if… Last time, it felt like I lost myself in that relationship. Like I only mattered in relation to him. I forgot who I was outside being his wife.'

And the mother of his unborn child. The pregnancy…the way that had taken over her body and mind, turned her into someone else, she *knew* that had affected her mindset too. Then losing the baby…

She'd felt out of control in her own life. As if nothing was her decision any longer. Everything that happened to her was caused by outside forces—Josh, the media, her body… everything and everyone except her own mind.

That was what she'd been searching for when she'd left. Autonomy. The chance to make her own decisions and decide who she wanted to be for herself.

And she'd done a pretty good job, as far as she was concerned.

But was it enough?

The hole in her heart that had started to fill when she'd reconnected with Josh in Iceland whispered perhaps not.

Melody seemed to understand. 'I know that when you've reached the point you have in life—you're successful on your own, you set your own rules, you've found your own self and you have your freedom to live however you want—it's hard to admit that you want something else. And even harder to take a risk on it when it might not turn out for the best. But all that means something else too, you realise.'

Winter blinked up at Melody. 'What? What does it mean?'

'It means you know you can survive.' Melody gripped Winter's shoulders and held her gaze. 'You've done it before, remember? You know you have the power to pick yourself up and start again and be *magnificent*. If you don't try again with Josh, you might always regret it. And if it falls apart, it will probably hurt like hell. But none of that changes a bit of who you are, you see. You're Winter de Holland, and you will be *amazing* with or without him. Nobody can take that away from you unless you let them.'

The words echoed in Winter's mind until

they were the only thing she could hear. Not the traffic outside the window, or the rattling trolley going past outside the room.

Nobody can take that away from you unless you let them.

She'd found her true self now. She could cling onto that. She wouldn't give it up.

She wouldn't let them take it. Not this time.

She was stronger than that now.

'The only thing that matters is what will make you happier right now and has the potential for greater happiness in the future,' Melody said. 'Okay?'

Winter nodded, dazed by her revelations. 'Okay. I…yeah. Okay.'

There was a knock on the door and Jenny popped her head around to tell them that their last interview of the day was ready at last. Winter made her way back to her seat, hoping she could still remember enough of the talking points to get through the interview.

Because suddenly her mind was overflowing with *other* things to think about.

And a decision she had to make.

Graham sounded surprised to hear from him late on a weekday afternoon, Josh thought. Or perhaps just surprised to hear from him at all. He hadn't been the best at staying in touch lately. And he hadn't called at all since everything with Winter in Iceland hit the news.

'How're things going in Holly Wood?' Graham pronounced it as two words as always, a not-so-subtle reminder that the world Josh lived in wasn't the same as the rest of them.

'Same old, same old,' Josh replied.

'Heard you had a run-in with your ex.' His brother always had been one to get straight to the heart of the matter. 'That what you're calling about?'

'Partly,' Josh admitted. 'It's not…we're not…' He sighed. 'Liam told me to call you.'

Graham barked a laugh. 'Did he? Got tired of dealing with your shit and decided to palm you off on family at last?'

'Not exactly.' Josh frowned as he tried to figure out exactly why Liam *had* wanted him to talk to his brother. 'It was just…we were talking about love.'

'Drunk, were you?'

'One solitary glass of bourbon, I promise you.'

Graham groaned. 'Talking about love sober? This must be serious. Hang on.'

Josh heard his brother calling out to Ashley, telling her he was going to take the call outside. With beer. The screen door slammed and the creaking of wood and scrape of the runners told him Graham was sitting on the old swing seat on the porch, even though it couldn't be that warm out there yet, at this time of year.

'Okay, I'm listening,' Graham said. 'Tell me everything.'

'You don't have time for everything,' Josh hedged.

'I'm your big brother,' Graham replied. 'I'll make time.'

Josh hesitated for a moment. And then he started to talk.

The story came easier this time than it had with Liam, perhaps because he was getting more used to telling it. Graham needed more background too. He'd been there for the fall-out of Winter leaving the first time, so all of that was old news. But their trip to Iceland, how it had come about and his feelings about it, all weighed in to the story.

He finished up by recounting his conversation with Liam over bourbon the day before.

'And he told you to call me?' Graham said.

'Yep. Any idea why?'

Graham sighed. 'Because your friend knows you well enough to have realised that you're an idiot. And there are certain truths you're only ever going to believe from the horse's mouth.'

Josh ignored the idiot comment—that was just par for the course with brothers, right?

'What truths?'

'You think true love should be easy? That Mom and Dad had the perfect marriage? That me and Ashley do?' Incredulity coloured Graham's voice.

'Don't you?' Josh countered. 'I've seen you two together. You *are* a perfect match.'

'I don't deny it,' Graham said. 'There's no other woman in the world for me, just like I don't think there's ever going to be anyone for Mom now that Dad has gone.'

'So I'm right.' Josh couldn't explain the slight disappointment at realising his brother was agreeing with him.

'No. You're wrong.' Graham laughed. 'And the most ridiculous thing is, you can't even see why, can you?'

'I suppose you're going to enlighten me.' No way Josh was admitting to not knowing, though.

'You think perfect is the same thing as easy,' Graham said. '*That's* where you're wrong.'

Josh blinked, letting the words settle, but stayed silent.

'Just because we're a perfect match, it doesn't mean Ashley and me don't work on our marriage every single day,' Graham went on. 'And if you think we don't have fights or disagreements…well, you *clearly* weren't here for the Great Dishwasher Row of four Thanksgivings ago is all I'm saying. Or any of the other hundreds of things we've disagreed about over the years.'

'Disagreements are normal,' Josh said. 'Even I know that. But underneath them…' Surely, underneath the petty stuff, the surface stuff, there had to be something more solid. Something that told a person that everything would be all right. A certainty that took away the constant fear.

'Underneath them everything is even harder,' Graham said soberly. 'The thing is, Josh, every moment you're with another person is a choice. Marriage doesn't change that. Every single day you wake up married to someone you still have to decide to *choose* them. To keep loving them. To stay by their side. To work as a team. True love isn't everything suddenly going smoothly because you said some words in front of a priest. It's deciding every day to make it work. To stick it out. To keep trying. Because the day you give up is the day it's all over.'

It was as if Josh blinked and clarity flowed over him.

Winter had given up on them when she'd walked away. But he'd given up too.

She'd accused him of always trying to fix everything, but that was only because it was easier than trying to understand it. To be there and feel her pain with her. To realise that there were things he might need to change—about himself, his life, his expectations.

He'd bought into the lie of the happy ever after. That once he'd put that ring on her finger everything would be plain sailing. And when it wasn't he'd pulled away. He'd *known* she was unhappy and because he didn't know how to fix it he'd pulled away.

Because it was easier to accept failure if he could blame it on something other than himself. On their schedules, or the miscarriage, or the press.

The truth was, he hadn't fought hard enough. He hadn't been the man she needed.

But now…now he needed to ask himself. Was he ready to be that man?

Because if he wasn't, then Winter was right to walk away again.

'Some days love is easy, some days it's hard,' Graham went on, unaware of Josh's sudden epiphany. 'The only thing I know for sure is that it's worth fighting for on *all* the days.'

'I think… I think I need to talk to Winter.'

He could almost hear Graham's smile down the phone. 'I think you're right, little brother.'

CHAPTER FOURTEEN

WINTER HAD SPENT a whole afternoon being primped, prodded, dressed and made up by the team Jenny had organised to get her ready for the awards ceremony that evening, and she hadn't even noticed half of it. Her mind was still focused on her conversation with Melody the day before. And what it meant for her future.

Josh would be at the awards tonight, even if they weren't going together any more. It would be her first time seeing him in person since Iceland, and she couldn't imagine making it through the whole evening without some sort of awkward conversation between them.

An awards ceremony red carpet was the last place she wanted to talk about her failure at a relationship with her ex, and she wasn't sure the afterparty would be a better location either. But they *did* need to talk.

She owed him some explanation. And a say in what happened next between them too.

And if he walked away... Melody was right. She'd survive. She'd *thrive*.

If she had to.

By the time the stylist was pushing a heavy emerald ring onto the finger of Winter's right hand, her hands were shaking with nerves.

I'm not ready for this.

But it was happening anyway.

At least she had the drive to the awards venue to get her nerves under control. Thanking everyone involved in making her look presentable for the night ahead, Winter took a quick glance in the mirror on her way to the door, still surprised to see herself looking so different to how she'd been when she'd dressed that morning. Then, with a last wave goodbye, she headed for the door.

The black limo waiting outside had the back door already open for her, a driver standing beside it as she climbed in. She thanked him, settled into her seat as the door shut behind her—and then screamed.

'What are you doing here?' She clutched a hand to her chest as she stared at Josh, sitting across the way from her.

'I needed to talk to you.' He shrugged.

'This seemed like the best way to get some privacy tonight.'

The old fears reared up again before Winter could stop them. 'Except now we're showing up at my awards ceremony together and—'

'I'll stay in the car,' Josh promised. 'We'll go round the block again and I'll get out later. Or I won't go at all. Whatever. I don't care. I just need to talk to you.'

'I... I wanted to talk to you too,' she admitted. 'So this isn't actually the worst idea in the world.'

'No, that remains sending two people on a date to a penis museum,' Josh joked, and Winter couldn't help but laugh.

'What did you want to say to me?' she asked.

Josh reached across and took her hand, the one with the heavy emerald ring, in his. He bit down on his lower lip, his gaze searching hers before he started to talk.

'I wanted to tell you...losing you again this last week or so has been hell. I tried to tell myself that it was for the best, that if something was this hard it just couldn't be meant to be. But I was wrong, I can see that now.' He sucked in a deep breath before continuing. 'I realised I was making the same mistakes

I made when we were married. Every time things got hard then, especially with your pregnancy and everything that followed... I tried to fix it. To make things easy again. And when I couldn't... I pulled away, because I felt like a failure.'

'You didn't fail us,' Winter interjected. 'My body did.'

Josh shook his head. 'No. You needed me— not to fix things, but to just be there, to be your husband. To choose every day to stay by your side because I loved you and being with you was worth every bit of pain we went through. But I didn't. I took jobs I didn't need to take, I spent most of my time away from you, because I couldn't forgive myself for the pain I was putting you through.'

Winter swallowed, her throat tight and her eyes burning. 'Josh...'

He squeezed her hand. 'Let me...let me get through this first, yeah? I've been thinking about this for days, and I want to make sure I get it all out.'

Winter nodded, and he continued.

'When you left me...part of me knew I deserved it. That's why I never fought for you, never tried to win you back. I let you go because I deserved to be without you,' he said.

'I told myself that it wasn't meant to be. That we'd bought into the fairy tale because of the media and all the talk about us. That if it was *really* true love it wouldn't be so hard. But I realise now, love has nothing to do with easy or hard. It's both.'

'I think you're right,' Winter said.

He flashed her a smile, but then his face turned serious again. 'I was using perfection as an excuse. A reason to stay away from you, so I didn't have to accept how badly I'd failed—last time, and this time, in Iceland.'

Winter frowned. 'How could you possibly have failed this time? *I* was the one who said we needed to deny the story. *I* gave up on us.'

'I failed because I never told you the truth,' Josh said. 'I went along with the idea that we were just trying a casual thing, to find closure, but that was never true for me. I didn't have the courage to tell you then what I need to tell you now. I love you. I never stopped loving you. I never *will* stop loving you. And I will wake up every morning for the rest of my life and choose you, no matter how hard it gets.'

Winter stared at him, the impossibility of it all battering against the optimism her conversation with Melody had given her.

'You can't mean that.'

'Why not?'

'Because…you want things! Things like marriage and kids and a picture-perfect life that I can't give you. That I don't think I even want these days!'

He shook his head. 'I don't need any of that. Our relationship won't be perfect, but it will be ours, and that's all that matters to me. If we—*we*—decide we want kids down the line, then we'll talk about that. About adopting or fostering or whatever works for us. But none of it is a dealbreaker for me. It never was.'

Her head was spinning too much to make sense of it all. And as much as she wanted to jump, to take the risk and be there with him, she had to be clear about everything first.

'Josh, I'm not the woman you fell in love with, remember? I'm harder and sadder and more independent and—'

'You're you,' Josh said simply. 'And I love you.'

And in that moment Winter knew exactly what she had to do.

It was as simple and as risky as that, Josh realised as he spoke the words. He'd put his heart on the line, and now all he could do was wait to see if she felt the same way.

Her green eyes were unreadable, her hand still in his. The limo came to a halt and he knew he was out of time.

Reluctantly, he let go of her hand. 'Go on. You go ahead. I'll go round the block a time or two and come back in a bit, once you're inside. We can talk more later, when we have some privacy.'

Winter stared at him for a long moment, those green eyes almost as bright as the emerald on her hand. 'I don't need privacy for what comes next,' she said finally. 'Come on.'

He blinked at her and opened his mouth, but before he could ask any more questions she'd swung her legs out of the open limo door, grabbed his hand and pulled him out behind her.

Josh had stood on a hundred or more red carpets in his career, but the flashing of bulbs and the shouted questions had never felt more intimidating than they did now, following Winter, unsure of what was going to happen next.

They hadn't agreed anything, had they? He'd put his heart on the line, but he still didn't know what was in hers. What she wanted.

'Josh! Winter! Are you two here together tonight?' one of the reporters called out as they made their way to the area where they'd pause for photos and answer a few questions.

Winter ignored him, so Josh did too.

Finally, she stopped in front of the crush of cameras, turning and smiling and posing just like she was supposed to. Josh stood back and watched, wanting her to have this moment in the sun, basking in her achievement. This was *her* night, and he wouldn't do anything that would take that from her.

But when she beckoned for him to join her he went and stood at her side, beaming proudly as they had photos taken together.

'Winter, are you and Josh here tonight as a couple?' a different reporter asked.

Winter flashed Josh a small secret smile and his heart felt as if it stopped as he waited to hear her answer.

'I'm here tonight to celebrate my film, *Another Time and Place*,' Winter said, her voice strong and clear. 'To celebrate the achievements of every person who worked on it, who gave their heart and soul to it, and who will

equally share in the glory if I win best director tonight—or even if I don't.'

'But you and—' someone started to inter-
rupt.

Winter held up a hand to stop them. '*But*,'
she said, 'it was brought to my attention recently by someone that I admire very much
that, since the film is all about second chances
in love, about taking chances even when you
know how big the risk really is, and how bad
the pain can be when things go wrong, it's
only right to talk about my own journey to
accepting the power of second chance love.'

She held them all in the palm of her hand
now, each reporter hanging on her every
word. Josh watched her proudly and tried to
hold back any fears about what she was about
to say.

'I've been asked often while working on
this project, why showing second chance love
matters in film. I talked about the importance
of representation, about how the characters
were more mature, how they knew themselves better, that sort of thing. And I stand
by all of it. But one thing I've learned over
the past few weeks is just how *brave* second
chance love is. And that's the message of my

movie, the message I'm sending out there to everyone watching tonight.

'Falling in love is scary. Giving your heart to someone else to hold is always, always a risk. And it's so easy not to take it. To hold back and protect ourselves from the heartache we know could come. Especially when we've been there before, we've already experienced the pain. We want to save ourselves from ever going through that again.

'But I'm here to tell you that it *is* worth the risk. Even if it hurts. Even if it goes wrong. Love is worth fighting for, every single day. It's worth every chance. Because sometimes you'll find your happily ever after—or even just a happily for now. And *that* is worth *everything*.'

A huge cheer went up from the surrounding crowd as she finished speaking and the camera flashbulbs went crazy. But Josh didn't notice any of it really.

All he could see was Winter. Winter smiling at him. Winter, beautiful in her gown. Winter, glowing with happiness and potential.

Winter, ready to take a second chance on love. On *him*.

She stepped closer and stretched up on her toes to kiss him, her arms wrapping around his neck. And Josh knew in that moment that she was completely right. Even if their love was never perfect, or easy, or anything else he'd thought it needed to be, it would always, always be worth fighting for.

EPILOGUE

CAMERA BULBS WERE flashing again as Winter sat down to another press conference, this time for her new movie—one she'd both directed *and* starred in for the first time. For a moment she felt as if she'd flashed back in time to two years ago, to that press conference after the award nominations had been announced. The one where she'd been blindsided by the fact she'd be spending a week in Iceland with her ex-husband.

Winter smiled, more to herself than for the cameras. If she'd only known then what she knew now...

A hand took hers as Josh sat down in the chair beside her and she turned her smile at him instead—knowing from the flashes that the cameras were going crazy at the signs of affection between the two of them.

She didn't care.

Something she'd learned over the last two

years—and learned the hard way, through trial and error, she'd admit—was that the cameras and the people behind them would see what they wanted to see, whatever she did. She couldn't control that. Just like she couldn't decide what Josh wanted from their relationship. Or how her body reacted to certain things.

What she *could* do—and what she now worked hard to do—was focus inward.

She put boundaries in place around her time and energy with the press, with social media and with the fans. She showed them her true, authentic self—and stopped worrying about what they actually saw, and whether it was the same thing.

Josh had put the work in too—although with him it had less to do with the press and more to do with their relationship. That was where the real effort went, for both of them.

The night they'd agreed to try again—the night she'd taken home the award for best director for *Another Time and Place,* and they'd fallen into bed the moment they'd got home from the afterparty and not left it except for food and bathroom breaks for three days—they'd talked, in between everything else, and come up with…not rules but a new guide for their relationship. The fact that she'd agreed to call it a relationship was, she'd thought at the time, a pretty good start.

Now, every day, they took time out to talk—to check in on each other's thoughts and feelings before they built up too much. They communicated far more than they ever had the first time around, and so much more honestly. They stopped guessing what the other wanted and started telling each other what they needed.

It didn't solve every problem, and God knew they still got it wrong sometimes. But every day they kept their promise to each other.

They chose to be together. They chose to find a way to make it work.

As for her body... Winter wasn't sure she'd ever fully trust it again, after the way it had betrayed her. But she'd learned to appreciate all the things it could do, rather than focusing on what it couldn't. Taking care of it—rather than just training or dieting for a role, or to fit into a dress—in a loving, mindful way, seemed to make a difference. She rested when she needed to rest and ate ice cream when she needed to eat ice cream. It worked for her.

In fact, it all did. She controlled what she could, communicated where she needed and let the rest go.

It felt amazing.

'Winter! How did it feel to get to boss Josh around on set for this movie?' The first question from the gathered throng of reporters earned a laugh, and Winter smiled before answering it.

'Lucky for me, Josh is a professional,' she replied. 'And when you're making a movie that's what you need more than anything. It didn't take us too long to figure out a way to make it work—and keep our home life off set.' No need to mention the time they'd had an argument about *someone* not putting an appointment on the calendar, gone to work in a bad mood, then been caught making up in the props trailer later that afternoon...

'Josh, same question for you, really,' another reporter called out. 'How did it feel being directed by Winter?'

Josh squeezed her hand before letting go and answering. 'My life is always better when I listen to her,' he joked, earning a laugh from the gathered reporters. 'No, seriously. We approached this movie the same way we approach our relationship, every day. We start with a commitment to put the work in to make it the best we can and go from there.'

That got 'Aww's from the audience, and

Winter ducked her head to hide what she suspected was a rather besotted smile.

The questions about the movie kept coming, finally shifting from their relationship to the actual film, and its chances come awards season. They took turns answering them, working in sync in a way she'd never imagined they could have again.

A way she'd never take for granted after all it had taken to get them there.

Finally the press conference started to wind down, and from the wings Winter's new assistant signalled the last question.

'What's next for you two?' the chosen reporter asked. 'Straight into another project? Together or separately? Or are you going to take some time off?'

Winter and Josh shared a glance. 'Definitely some time off,' Josh said, and she was sure that everyone in the room had to be able to hear the heat in his voice. 'Together.'

At least they didn't know all the things he'd promised to do to her during that time off, several of them involving her wearing her red bikini—and then not wearing it. Although if the heat in her cheeks was any indication, her blush might give some of them away.

She cleared her throat and smiled brightly

at their audience, while lightly slapping Josh's thigh under the table.

'We're off to Costa Rica,' she said. 'We've got a wedding to go to.'

'Yours?' someone called eagerly, as a hum of speculation filled the room.

Josh laughed. 'Not this time, I'm afraid.' He reached for her hand again under the desk— her left hand—and Winter felt him run a finger across her ring finger, over the spot where her wedding ring used to sit.

Where, just last night, he'd placed another ring, a new one. One he'd had designed just for who they were now, not who they had been.

They'd agreed she wouldn't wear it today or it would be all anyone would ask about, so it hung on a chain under the high neck of her dress until the press conference was over and she could wear it again.

There was no rush. They'd tell the world when they were ready.

After all, they had the rest of their lives to look forward to.

Together.

* * * * *

*Look out for the next story in the
Dream Destinations duet,
coming soon!*

*And if you enjoyed this story, check out
these other great reads from
Sophie Pembroke*

Baby on the Rebel Heir's Doorstep
Their Second Chance Miracle
Vegas Wedding to Forever

All available now!